ALSO BY STEVE BERMAN

Trysts
Vintage

SECOND
THOUGHTS

STEVE BERMAN

Published by LETHE PRESS
Copyright © 2008 by Steve Berman.

www.lethepressbooks.com

ISBN 1-59021-028-X / 978-1-59021-028-4

Full publication history of the stories contained in this volume can be found on page
174, consituting a continuation of this copyright page. No one monstrous
was hurt in the making or publishing of this manuscript.

Book Design by INKSPIRAL DESIGN
Cover Design by RYAN VANCE

In memory of Michael Carte

Odi et amo.

CONTENTS

*"I don't want realism. I want magic! Yes, yes, magic.
I try to give that to people. I do misrepresent things.
I don't tell truths. I tell what ought to be truth."*

—Blanche DuBois

BITTERSWEET

THE BOYS ORDERED the greatest hot drink ever meant for a glass: Vietnamese coffee. The base of ivory condensed milk. The top of so-brown-it's-black chicory coffee. The boys marveled at the dichotomy. Only one coffee shop in Philly offered their favorite. Posters and flyers covered nearly every wall. The latest single from the Red Caps, a remix of *Hungry Like the Wolf*, way overplayed, hung in the air.

Dault watched Jerrod tip his glass, the lip pale from steam. Doughy and pale, Jerrod didn't like to break margins. He must have been the first kid to color within the lines. The sort who regretted spooning peanut butter from the jar first.

"Would you date a gingerbread man?" Dault asked. The distraction afforded him the chance to plunge a spoon into his own glass and stir.

"Being diabetic..." Jerrod's forehead creased, making him doubly serious. "I have you anyways."

Dault drank for several seconds to earn a murky mustache. Anything to make his boyfriend grin. It worked. "Someone made a cartoon of the fairy tale. Posted it on YouTube." He wiped his lips clean with the back of his hand.

"That the one with a wolf?"

"Was a fox, not a wolf. Drink your coffee. Would you rather date a wolf or a gingerbread man?" Dault had often wondered what kissing a wolf would be like. Wolves kiss first and ask permission later. Or maybe never even ask permission.

"Are you dumping me so I can date make-believe people?"

Dault didn't dare hesitate to answer. Jerrod had a list of worries, more than any other guy he'd ever dated. *Foot falling off* had to be at the top, but the way he would dare Dault to break up with him suggested *Getting dumped* was high on the list. Jerrod's hazel eyes flickering on the table top, as if he were suddenly consulting that list, made Dault regret the joke. "No," he said carefully, "just curious."

Jerrod nodded and smiled. "I think a wolf would snore. Well, maybe I'd date the wolf from the little pigs story. The one who goes after Riding Hood's too straight. And didn't the gingerbread kid run away?"

"Yeah, the whole 'Run, run, as fast as you can!' bit. But I think he'd hitchhike these days. Maybe be all skater on a biscotti."

Jerrod's crutches began to slide down the wall, tearing at band flyers printed on jam-red paper. Dault caught them before they clattered. He'd trip over them, like he had when they first met in Mr. Corlen's seventh period History class. Jerrod had looked so guilty that Dault knew he'd say yes when asked out on a date.

"Why'd he run away?" Jerrod finally took a sip. Dault knew he'd never drink the entire glass. He worried about his blood sugar.

"A pair of dykes made him. They wanted a kid—"

"They couldn't adopt?" asked Jerrod.

"I was adopted."

"Liar. You look like your mom."

"She was adopted too. We came as a package."

"I wish I wasn't related to my folks."

Dault knew that any moment Jerrod would spiral down into some serious moping; his boyfriend's home life was the Unmentionable Topic to be avoided at all costs. But lately, Jerrod had been dropping hints, little *mals mots*. That a bad divorce didn't prevent bad genes.

"I'll adopt you." Dault reached out and ruffled Jerrod's thin blond hair.

Jerrod tried to duck out of the way. "You just want to make me forget about tomorrow."

The flight to Indianapolis with his father. Surgery the very next day. If all went well there'd be weeks of physical therapy. If things went bad, there'd be a lot of therapy. Losing a foot meant all sorts of therapy. Dault told himself not to envision Jerrod trapped in a wheelchair.

"I want to see you walk off the plane."

"Hobble. I'll still have the crutches." Jerrod pushed the glass away from him. "I don't want to go."

"I don't want you to go either." But Dault did. He wanted a whole Jerrod, not a partial. He didn't know if he could be with an amputee. That would make him an awful person—I mean, only the worst guy in the world would dump his disabled boyfriend, right?

They had slept together a few times, and it had been awkward. Awkward sex because of blood flow and neuropathy; Jerrod couldn't really get hard. So Dault had to lie back and let Jerrod do things to him. It felt selfish and he found himself making tiny jokes to keep from being anxious.

Afterwards had been just as awkward. Dault would drift off and then suddenly wake, terrified he had kicked Jerrod's bad foot. He would feel his muscles cramp against the task of remaining still for hours while Jerrod's feverish body made the bed feel like an oven.

"Perhaps I can run away," Jerrod said.

"As fast as you can?"

Jerrod nodded. "They really need to change the album. Has it been the same song?" He reached for his crutches. Dault noticed how the others in the coffee shop stared at Jerrod as he struggled to his feet. The protective boot looked enormous, like something an astronaut would wear.

"How did it end for the gingerbread boy?"

"You want another lie?" Dault asked.

"Sure."

"Happily ever after. Met a very handsome fritter and they ran off together."

"Just desserts?"

"I should smack you for that."

"A kiss instead." Dault wished he didn't have to ask.

=

DAULT WANDERED AROUND Philly for hours, trying not worry. Summertime should have been trips to the beach, dripping ice cream cones, exploring underneath the pier and making out in the shade. Not moping. The text message Jerrod sent him hours later didn't help. Jerrod's texts were always so perfect. Never an error, never any shorthand. They had once sat through a bad horror movie and texted back and forth and it took Jerrod three times as long to type his messages.

> *What if the gingerbread boy wasn't a victim? What if he was a lure? Dropped onto people's plates. He'd have folks chasing him, boys chasing him, and he'd run to that witch's house. The one also made of gingerbread. Think I'm wrong?*

Dault replied.

> *Relx every1 likes gbread how was the flight? Dont b worried luv ya. Maybe you should run, run as fast as you can.*

Dault groaned. He tried calling but Jerrod wouldn't pick up. That night he fell asleep with the open cell phone hot against his pillow.

=

BY THE END of the week, his mother hid the cell phone. She dangled the car keys in front of his face and told him to go out, take a long drive, get some sun and not worry why Jerrod had not returned calls, texts or emails in days. She threatened to spend his college savings on liposuction if he didn't listen.

She only gave him back the phone when he reasoned it wasn't safe to be out on the road without one. Cars break down. Curfews get broken. People get lost.

Like his boyfriend. He wondered if Jerrod had gone all cowardly and decided to end the relationship with silence. Or maybe he had decided to be a martyr—yes, Dault could imagine him doing that, deciding that Dault would be better off not dating a cripple. That word made him sick and ashamed.

He escaped to New Hope with its tidy streets filled with tourists and motorcycle gangs. The restaurants either charged nearly twenty dollars a dish or served hamburgers on paper plates. Leather shops and Wiccan stores and stained glass art.

He sat on the steps outside a tattoo parlor and watched the people walk past. He considered getting a bitter tattoo, something like *Bite me*. Or *Eat me*. He ended up smiling, trying to imagine where on his body would be most fun to get inked.

Three boys passed by. Their hair was spiked with product, their tanktops glaring white over tanned skin, shorts drooped below thin waistlines. Golden-brown skin. The last of the three met Dault's stare and actually turned around down the block to smile at him.

Later, he saw them across the street, entering the ice cream parlor. The third boy dawdled in the doorway a while, offered Dault a slight wave to which he couldn't help but smile. That same boy came out with two cones and ran across the street. A Volkswagen almost ran him down.

"Hey, you look sad." The boy had ginger-colored hair below the lighter streaks. He held out one of the cones. "Go on, take it."

Dault couldn't help but have his fingers brush the other boy's while gripping the waffle cone.

The boy sat down beside him without asking. "So are you browsing or buying?"

"What?" The ice cream tasted like a cinnamon stick that nipped the tip of his tongue.

"Just browsing the boys or looking to take one home?"

Dault blushed. "You bought me ice cream, not a ring."

The boy nodded. He had a chipped front tooth and bit at the scoops of ice cream. "Hang with us. Have some fun."

He felt his cell phone vibrate in the pocket of his cargo shorts. Jerrod's ring tone, Average Superstar's *Radiate*.

"See, someone wants you to come with us," said the boy who wore sandals and had painted his toenails jam-red.

He shouldn't ignore the phone. He'd never before. But in the hot sun the smell of cinnamon hung in the air about the boy, who bumped against him, and Dault told himself if he answered and it ended up being that painful conversation where Jerrod tells him he won't be coming back, at least, not to him, then he'd be left broken. Better to pretend the call never happened.

So when the boy offered a hand to help Dault to his feet, he took it and followed him across the street back to the boy's waiting friends. All their names began with R, but Dault couldn't allow himself to remember any of them, not least the ginger-haired boy. That would be something like dating.

By the afternoon, the four of them had walked along to the river. Dault worried about getting lost by the trees. The boy held his hand and guided him around birch and cherry until the path had disappeared. So had the others.

"Chase me," said the ginger-haired boy.

"No, I think I better get back." Dault's cell phone had chirped a few times. Jerrod had left a message.

The boy slapped him on the chest. "Bet you can't catch me." Then he started to run through the tree line. Dault watched him strip off his tanktop. His heart raced as if he were the one being chased. I shouldn't, he thought, but already he had begun to follow.

The way was marked with discarded clothes. A sandal. He saw only one. Shorts. He expected underwear, was curious whether it would be boxers or briefs, when a hand grabbed his arm, pulling him to the ground.

The ginger-haired boy rolled atop him and, without asking, kissed him hard. The tongue that worked its way past Dault's lips tasted sweet. He discovered the rest of the boy less so.

=

ON THE DRIVE back home to New Jersey, Dault listened to the voice message. Route 295 seemed deserted. He was hours late. He still smelled the other boy on his skin.

"Dault, he stole it." Jerrod's voice sounded so weak. Either he whispered or he could barely speak. "The gingerbread boy stole my foot." Nothing more. He tried replaying it but the message, the voice, had vanished. Maybe he had been so tired he pushed the wrong button. He caught himself beginning to swerve onto the shoulder and kicked the brakes. The tires squealed and he almost cracked his skull on the steering wheel.

His chest ached from where the seat belt restrained him. He put the car in park and decided that a good cry might be the best thing.

The porch light remained lit at his house. When he pushed the key into the lock, the wood around the doorknob cracked like stale pastry. He pushed a finger past sharp slivers and felt splinters bite.

On the bottom step of the hall staircase was the yellow pad where his mother wrote down phone messages.

Jerrod called. Twice. You got lucky. He felt sick that she had guessed right about spending the night with another boy.

In his bedroom, he threw his wallet on the desk. A scrap of paper, the receipt for the ice cream cone had the third boy's digits scrawled on it. The desktop computer, sleeping, rumbled to life.

New email blinked over the blurred desktop picture of Dault and Jerrod kissing. Blinked over their eyes, his closed, Jerrod's open and wary of the cell phone taking their picture inches away.

> *Hey, Dault,*
>
> *Sorry I have been out of touch. I had to have two surgeries in a row and been mostly sleeping. Guess now you can tease me about being a dope fiend. I have to tell you whatever they put in my IV was amazing stuff. No pain whatsoever.*
>
> *My foot's all wrapped tight. The doctor (he's this cool guy who's worked on the local football team... Does that make me an honorary athlete?) said I should be wiggling toes in no time. But no dancing. I don't dance, remember.*
>
> *Please, please forgive me. My father's only wanted me to rest.*
> *I must have made your mom crazy tonight with calls. She told me you went out. Please, please call me tomorrow. Hearing your sweet voice would make everything better.*
>
> *Love,*
>
> *A whole Jerrod*

Dault glanced at his cell phone. That creepy message. Had he imagined it? He rubbed his face and wished the whole day had been a hallucination.

He hit Reply.

Jerrod

Glad the surgery went okay. You need to relax and get better. Don't worry about dancing. I promise I won't ask you to dance.

Dault stopped typing out of fear what he'd write next. He thought about hiding behind some lies. Jerrod would never have to know about the gingerboy. Or would the phone ring again with his conscience on the line whispering to him? He didn't want it eating away at him.

I'll see you when you come back home.
D

He might not be the good boyfriend, a seventeen-year-old Prince Charming, but Dault swore he needn't be the villain. He wished though that he was made of sugar and spice and everything nice.

AUTHOR'S NOTE

TERRI WINDLING INVITED me to write a story for a young-adult-themed issue of the Journal of Mythic Arts. I agreed, of course, without much thought. I tend to do that a great deal. But as the deadline neared, I realized the story I'd been working on was nothing more than a patchwork of scenes without the needed narrative. I decided to write something different, even though I had two days time. Staring at the SurLaLune website, I closed my eyes and stabbed my finger at the screen—whatever fairytale my fingertip touched would be the inspiration for a story. I don't recommend this method. I was desperate. The link for "The Gingerbread Man" brought little relief; it's not a fairy tale at all but a mnemonic device for storytellers to entertain children. Despite digging deeper, I found little folklore about pastry on the loose.

The notion of a gingerbread boy did, though, summon a memory. At DragonCon 2002, I met a handsome guy who wore a complicated footcast and a gauzy shirt that stuck to his torso with sweat. His diabetes put his foot at risk and in a few days he'd visit a surgeon and see if he needed amputation. But he never seemed distraught. I fell for him. Despite my fear, while we lay in bed or as we showered, that I might take one wrong step and be the real reason why he lost his foot. Surgery saved the limb. But I lost him. He stopped writing, calling. Should I blame the many miles that separated us? Or perhaps my words failed to move him.

As for the ending, well, that's a dash of guilt over losing someone special. Sometimes the sweetest of words are not enough.

SECRETS OF THE GWANGI

TUCK KIRBEN HAD never hidden from danger once in his thirty-four years—not when he outrode a wild twister in the Kansas territory, not when that crazed Chinaman with the hatchet had wanted to settle a gambling score, and certainly not when an entire saloon had been ready to lynch him after learning what he'd done on the piano the very night before. But damn it, he now found himself hiding underneath a rock outcropping like a snake without its rattle and only half a fang.

From where he crouched, he couldn't see any of the *gwangi*, as T.J. called the fucking things, but Tuck knew they soared above, just waiting to pick him off like he was some scampering jackrabbit. Beads of sweat rolled down Tuck's body, and his unbuttoned, soiled shirt stuck to his chest and back like a second skin. Even as the sun set, the jungle valley held the heat like scorched Texas dirt. He cursed that map promising silver veins as thick as a man's arm, but if there was any ore down here, he doubted they'd ever live to find it. He wiped the brow beneath his wide-brimmed hat. Salt stung his eyes and sweat dripped onto the coarse paper as he scribbled in his journal. That old schoolmarm who'd done taught him letters would be all hobbled if she ever read his words.

He heard the crunch of gravel from behind him, reached for his pistol and nearly shot poor T.J. full of lead. He offered the vaquero a sorry grin of apology. Tuck had traveled down to Mexico looking to challenge the infamous Tiago Josue Sanz to a gunfight. He'd found the man holding court in a vast cantina. T.J. had pushed the painted whore off his knee and accepted the challenge. But first tequila. Though he'd been bottle sharp since knee high, Tuck had never drunk so much in all his days, matching the dreadfully handsome tawny-skinned devil glass for glass. Finally, somewhere between toasts to *el de atrás* and *ir a un entierro*, Tuck had found himself wanting to fuck T.J. more than shoot him. The vaquero had eyes like Spanish missionary chocolate, and his carefully groomed mustache ached to be messed by fierce lips. The painted stripe, red like fire, running down T.J.'s tight pants had taunted Tuck.

When they had stumbled out of the cantina together, full as ticks trying to walk, too stubborn to collapse, Tuck half-dragged, half-sweet-talked the Mexican back to the edge of town. Behind some sagebrush he fought him to the ground. Not with six-shooters but the red-hot iron unshucked from his wool pants. He tasted every inch of T.J., sucked down his *mecos* like marrow to a starving man. The stuff was fine as creamy gravy on Tuck's tongue. He made sure T.J. knew he could break any bronco, especially one who cussed as he moaned.

Afterward, well, there weren't any need for the gunfight. He stayed in town for a while till T.J.'s amigos began whispering and giving him steel glares. Tuck had been ready to silence them quick, but T.J. by then had found the old prospector's body and the map.

Shit. Tuck wished they'd never gone off looking for silver. Taking on a dozen thick-headed south-of-the-border hounds would be a heap better compared to these giant flying lizard-vultures.

"I scouted the area. Counted four in the sky." T.J. pulled off his sarape. His thick dark hair remained askew, and Tuck gently cleared the vaquero's forehead, which felt feverish. There weren't much water left in their canteens and only crumbs in their packs.

The gwangi ate proper on their horses. Tuck didn't think there'd be anything left of poor Stokes and Tana than cracked bones and iron shoes. He needed to find them some water to cool off in and drink. It would bring T.J.'s fever down. Then they could think straight and figure out a way to get out.

=

WILLIS PUT DOWN the yellowed sheets of paper gently, but a curled edge still broke loose on his workshop desk. He took out a handkerchief from his pocket and absently wiped his fingers clean.

"Genuine?"

The Mexican fellow, who'd been staring at the various armatures and half-made puppets, swung his head back to face Willis and nodded, almost violently, while beginning a chanted barrage of "yes" and "sí." He nervously clutched the battered leather satchel that had kept the journal safe for almost a century.

Willis took out his wallet. The act silenced the Mexican man, and then his eyes grew wide, no doubt in anticipation. Just how long after his phone call had he been waiting for some gringo to count out bills?

The story of the century only cost Willis eighty-three dollars. Or the greatest hoax. Not that it mattered. What else was making movies than a combination of both?

=

TUCK OFFERED THE last of his water to T.J. Together, their fingers held the canteen. He fought the urge to kiss away the drops that hung on T.J.'s lips and mustache. Now weren't the time for such things.

He cautiously looked out at the sky from underneath the rock. Plenty of clouds in the clear blue, but it looked anything but calm. Any one of those clouds could be hiding a hungry gwangi.

Still, they had to move while there was light. At night they could stumble through the jungle and miss a pond three feet from them. Tuck put away his journal. He hoped he'd have a chance to write more later. In one hand he held his shooting iron; in the other he took hold of T.J.'s sweaty palm.

=

WILLIS ARRIVED EARLY to his meeting with the studio executive. He paced near the receptionist who watched him warily out of the corner of her eye. Her fingers went *clickety-clack* on the typewriter keys. Normally, the sound comforted him—he always considered it a cunning echo of creative energy—but that afternoon he found the typing an uncomfortable staccato. He tried not to glare at her, worried she might think he was staring at her more-than-ample tits straining her fuzzy blouse.

The phone rang, and in one smooth motion the receptionist swept the receiver to her ear. "Yes, sir," she said. When she told Willis he could go in she didn't even look at him.

The studio executive's office had its own personal fogbank, not Thames murk but Chesterfield bluish-gray smoke drifting about the ceiling. Willis had never known the man not to have a hand- or mouthful of a cigarette.

"Thank you for seeing me—"

"Willis, are you trying to give me a heart attack?" The executive leaned back and stabbed at the front of his vest. Ashes flickered about his person.

"I don't understand."

"This *dreck*." The man slid a thick yellowed hand over the pages on his immense mahogany desk and sent them cascading over the edge in a magnificent paper waterfall into the wastebasket. "*The Valley Time Forgot*. Pfeh. I wish I could forget I read it."

"It's the queer thing, right? But this," Willis lifted his own copy of the screenplay, thirteen days of sweat and blood spent over the keys of his Remington, his thoughts consumed with imaging how metal wire and papier-mâché could bring the creatures to life. "This is guaranteed drive-in gold."

"You're fucking nuts, Willis, if you think anyone wants to see a movie about two faggot cowboys—"

"What about the ferocious pterodactyls?"

"More dinosaurs and less *faygelehs*. That's what makes a movie." The executive flicked open his gilded lighter, even though his last cigarette still smoldered at the corner of his mouth.

=

THIRTEEN YEARS AFTER the filming wrapped, the drive-ins of suburban New Jersey have gone the way of the dinosaur. UHF features the horror and fantastical films on Saturday and Sunday afternoons. Steve sits on the floor in the den, his friend Chucky close by, and watches the movie on the bulky console RCA television.

Steve holds one of the couch pillows in his lap, almost as if hiding behind it. Not that the monsters on the seventeen-inch screen are the least bit threatening, but lately he finds Chucky to be so. Or rather, his thoughts about Chucky. He turns back to the television and decides the movie would be a lot cooler if the handsome cowboy—who has the silly name of Tuck, which must have been just awful when the guy went to school—wouldn't bother so much with the girl. Yeah, Steve thinks, grabbing a handful of Fritos from the bowl by Chucky's knees, T.J. ought to have been a guy. Then the kissing part wouldn't be so bad. Not that Steve has ever kissed another boy, but he does wonder a lot about it, especially when he's around Chucky.

On the curved glass screen the cowboys begin to lasso the clay allosaurus. Chucky starts to laugh. His breath reeks of corn chips. "That's so gay."

Steve winces, and then, with a steadiness that surprises him, lifts a hand up in a pistol gesture. He takes aim at Chucky's handsome features and clicks his thumb. Bang.

=

ON THE MAKESHIFT studio lot, the dust settled to the earth minutes after the jeep stopped. Esteban looked over his shoulder and saw the loco American leap from where he had sat in the back, still clutching some sort of pole. Esteban didn't understand why he had to drive around in circles while men tried to rope the pole's end. But the movie business paid well.

In the passenger seat, Carlos laughed as the movie folk scrambled like busy ants. Esteban loved the sound of Carlos's deep laughter as it so often came before an embrace. Making sure no one watched, he reached over and firmly squeezed the crotch of his friend's denim jeans. Carlos favored him with a smile.

"Tonight," Esteban said, leaning in close, "let's steal away to the jungle set and pretend we are lost in their valley."

"What of the monsters?" The crazy American who had wielded the pole played with toy lizards, posing them for hours.

Esteban squeezed more and felt the reassuring firmness and heat beneath his palm. "I like some monsters." He kissed Carlos, tasting a bit of the road dirt in the man's mouth, but the grit did not last long. "Besides, we can play cowboy." He made sure to say the word in English, feeling it strange and wondrous on his lips.

AUTHOR'S NOTE

TABLE 1-1
d8 Tale's Veracity
Die Roll - Result

1 - Story is utterly true

2 - Some names may have been changed to protect the less innocent

3 - Happened to a friend of a friend

4 - Reminds you of an urban legend going around on the 'net

5 - Be suspicious of anything the author says

6 - Make saving throw or be convinced

7 - Artistic license may have been abused

8 - Story is a complete fabrication; libelous elements promise legal action

THIS HAPPENED WHEN I was twelve. Or maybe thirteen.

On the other side of the block lived Chucky G—. I'd known him soon after moving to the suburban neighborhood years ago. The inside of the G— house always had a peculiar odor, not so much unpleasant as noticeable. Every room had its mess, from the kitchen's Everfull Sink to the living room's clutter to Chucky's bedroom littered with clothes and sports crap. Chucky seemed the embodiment of his house too, his skin a shade darker than everyone else I knew, like unwashable grime, gangly, and a wide grin that promised playfulness.

Why Chucky wanted to play with little lead figures, faceted bits of rolling plastic, and books of endless charts and listings of monsters and magic never made sense. Chucky played football. Chucky sweated, had soiled armbands and socks and somewhere a jockstrap in the piles of his room.

During summer, we played all the time. Some nights Chucky's father, a man with a bristly mustache and a new job every month, would join us exploring dungeons or floating castles. Now and then we'd abandon swords and steeds for ray guns and jetpacks. But mostly it was just Chucky and me lounging around the bedroom or living room.

One afternoon, as sunlight played across the tired pale paint above the sofa, I decided there'd be no battles that day. Chucky's warrior, a hero to us both, had come to a new kingdom and found himself greeted by the young and beautiful princess.

We both sat there, nursing Cokes in sweating cans. Chucky and me, not the warrior and the princess; they sipped wine from heavy golden goblets.

I am so happy that you graced my castle, Sir T—. I have long heard of your exploits.

Chucky wiped his mouth but the few fine hairs he'd achieved on his upper lip remained damp. Thanks for the invite, Princess S—. I am tired from defeating the Forest of Spiders and could use a bath and a soft bed for the night.

I stifled a laugh. Chucky looked like he never bathed but his character craved soapy water after every dungeon crawl. I mock-tipped the soda can towards my friend. Of course. My servants will prepare for all your needs.

All of them? Chucky had a strange smile on his face.

I remembered seeing that expression before. Had it been last week? We'd been upstairs, playing a spy game, and Chucky's femme fatale had offered my agent a handjob. That had given me pause, abandoning the storyline. What was a handjob, I'd wondered, trying to remember if it was some martial arts technique covered in the handbook. Finally, a bit embarrassed that Chucky knew something I didn't, I asked him.

Chucky had laughed a while. It's when a girl grabs your boner and yanks it until you're done.

Oh. *The percentile dice in my hand had tumbled down onto the floor. I never looked at the result. My face had felt hot. The sex between my spy and the femme fatale had lasted less than a minute or two, as Chucky described it, before I was off to kill the Soviet mole. Later, during the five-minute walk home, I'd used the rulebook to hide the stiffness in my crotch.*

I found myself saying back, Of course, good knight. Whatever you wish that is within my power to grant.

You're alone here?

I nodded solemnly. A dragon came and slaughtered many. My father, the king...his last proclamation promised my hand to whoever killed the beast.

A dragon? I'm glad I came here. Tomorrow I will slay the monster. You would save us all?

Chucky put down his Coke on the dun-colored carpet. He stood up and drew an imaginary +3 bastard sword. Only if you agree to marry me. *Chucky's brown eyes met mine.*

I swallowed hard, feeling a bit unsteady. Where and why was our acting headed? I normally second-guessed his every move during a game— he always wanted mayhem. This was something new.

More than the princess spoke. You want me?

The hero of Iris Lane nodded, surprising the princess by moving forward, straddling where she sat on the old velour sofa.

I could smell the sweetness of the cola on Chucky's breath. My asthmatic lungs seized for a moment and I wondered if I'd have an attack right before... before something happened. I realized how hard my dick was. I worried that Mrs. G— would come home hours early from her nursing job to find us... I didn't dare imagine how she'd find us.

Aren't you lonely?

The princess nodded several times. I'd been lonely so long, even when among friends I'd felt outside their camaraderie.

Chucky looked down at himself. I glanced down his T-shirt to jeans with holes at the knee.

The knight moved an inch closer until that same leg bumped against my hand.

All my needs? *Whether I heard the knight say it or merely imagined he had didn't matter. Another bump with the leg. The fullness of Chucky's jeans seemed to widen.*

I looked up at his face, at thin lips pressed together tight, at brown eyes I could not read.

My hand trembled as it pressed against Chucky's crotch. Would her slender fingers have slipped past the knight's enchanted armor as easily as I unzipped the Wrangler jeans' fly? The glimpse of pale underwear underneath stopped me.

Chucky took my hand and guided me inside where it was so warm. The hero moaned slightly.

Something wet slicked one of my fingertips. The sensation made the length of my arm shudder. Chucky leaned further against me, as I slipped my entire hand inside his pants. I watched how the muscles in Chucky's unwashed neck tensed when I stroked down. He'd swallow when my fingers slid up.

Yes. Chucky hissed the word into many syllables. The hero then grunted.

I felt warmth pooling around his fingers. A few more tugs and Chucky shuddered and backed off awkwardly as a coated hand struggled out of his pants.

Damn. Chucky zipped himself back up, the hero repairing his armor chink by chink after his latest adventure.

I sat there, looking at the amazing mess covering my hands. I didn't know what to do other than marvel at the stuff. One soft thumb slid a measure around on my palm like a third-level fortune teller, but I couldn't discern whatever message the cooling semen offered.

You better go.

Yeah. I went to the tiny first-floor bathroom and ran cold, cold water over my hand, congealing the come into lumps that washed down the drain. I wiped away the last traces on the slightly soiled hand towel that smelled far worse than the house.

Later, in bed, I stared at my palm looking for some trace of Chucky. But there was none. I'd washed the hand in hot water until the skin became pink. Only then did I bring the tip of my tongue to the soft pads. My imagination offered a taste: salty like sweat, acrid like dirt, lacquered smooth like Pearl Drops. I'd once spent all my allowance on a tiny bottle of Pearl Drops in the hopes that the other kids would see a bright smile and admire me. But the drops did nothing.

I envied how everyone at school liked Chucky's gap-toothed smile as if it were magic.

KISS

WITHOUT AIR-CONDITIONING, THE temperature inside the car racing down the highway felt twenty degrees hotter than the surrounding desert. Beneath the sweaty t-shirt he wore, Mike could feel his back sliding against the seat. His roommate sat behind the wheel with one arm out the window catching the breeze. Blond, shirtless, and tan, eyes concealed behind mirrored sunglasses, Ryan did not seem the least bit diminished by the heat.

"Do you think Tom's a top or bottom?" he asked, glancing over at Mike.

Tom was supposed to be one of the features at tonight's party. A junior with hopefully more than a 4.0 average. Maybe seven inches. "Does it matter?" Mike had known Ryan to convince the most adamant top to beg with his knees up around his ears.

Ryan grinned, his smile perfect except for a chipped front tooth. He told everyone it had been a skateboarding injury from years back. After several shots of tequila, though, Ryan confided that during winter break an ex had hit his face with a fridge door.

He'd met Ryan in their freshman year at U of A. Both shared the same floor of the dorm but separate rooms to start. Then Ryan's roommate had told the RA he wouldn't share space with a faggot. Mike had grown up with a pair of "aunts" who helped raise him, so he had no problem volunteering to switch rooms.

Their first kiss had happened while sitting on the floor. Ryan had a few friends over to share some of Canada's finest. Mike turned and saw Ryan waiting for him with the lit end of the blunt in his mouth. He leaned in and touched lips with Ryan, opening his mouth a moment later. THC-laced smoke linked them. Ryan's fingers tapped an echo of the rising heartbeat against the back of his neck.

Mike had never before tasted boy or drug and found the two flavors to his liking.

Ryan swerved the car to avoid the flattened carcass of a rabbit lying in the middle of the road.

"Chupacabra."

"Huh?" Mike glanced over his shoulder at the road behind him.

"That's what killed the rabbit." Ryan lifted his gaze to the rearview mirror.

"Looked like a Goodyear going sixty-five was to blame."

"Nope, the chupacabra," Ryan said.

"What the hell is that?" Mike peeled his back from the car seat.

"The Mexican goat-sucker."

Mike looked at Ryan, expecting to see a stupid grin. The handsome face didn't disappoint him. "Is that like a Dirty Sanchez?"

"How come I'm from California and I've heard of it?"

Mike shrugged. Now and then he felt diminished being around Ryan. "Like every boy from Tucson has."

"They're aliens."

"Wait, I thought you said they're Mexicans. How can they be both?"

"Maybe they're illegal aliens?"

"That's so bad," Mike said with a groan.

"They're supposed to be these creatures that drain the blood from animals." Ryan dropped his voice low, as if to be spooky. "People, too, on occasion. They look like spiny little gray men with tongues like a frog, 'cept that's how they drink, like through a straw."

"Right." Mike stared out into the desert. It looked so empty. Lonely was the word that came to mind. "So you've bought from this guy before, right?"

"Yeah." Ryan looked away from the road for a moment to pick through jewel cases in the bin between the seats. "Here, the Red Caps. Track four."

He slid the CD into the dashboard. Harsh lyrics that blended with industrial beat filled the car.

Ryan tapped the wheel with his slender fingertips in time to the music. "Cruz deals the best shit. Tonight's party will be made by what we bring back."

"Cool," Mike said though he didn't want to rush their return to campus. At the party, he'd have to compete for Ryan's attention.

Ryan tapped the brake pedal once before turning onto a dirt side road. Clouds of reddish dust blew from around the tires.

"Where do you know about all this shit?"

"What, the peyote? Mescalito?" A chuckling Ryan shook his head. "My brother was kicked out of pharmacy school."

Mike knew that real life had worse things than bogeymen. Envy. Want. Loneliness. These sudden and new sensations frightened him— not superstition. "No, the chuba..."

"Chup-acabra. That's from Alvaro."

"I thought you said this guy's name is Cruz."

Ryan nodded. "Alvaro was this kid I met back in high school. Tutored me in Spanish. Was the first uncut cock I ever saw."

Mike laughed, trying not to think how long it had taken him to lose his virginity. The event, much fumbling in the back of the girl's Jeep, was not worth bragging. Ryan always had better stories than he could muster. "Did you get an 'A' on the tests?"

"B minus. Just to make sure I got weekly visits. Still, I was his best *mayate* pupil."

"Just never tell me exactly how many guys you've done. I don't want to be scared."

"Aww, poor Mikey." Ryan's tone stung. "Maybe tonight you can work on catching up to me."

They'd slept together a few times after becoming roommates. But Ryan's eye and mouth wandered a lot, and Mike had no choice but to graduate to best friend when it was clear that being boyfriend wasn't an option. The last time they'd done anything was after Jell-O shots. They'd woken up in bed together, mostly clothed, and sipped water from a bottle together to rehydrate. Mike had spilled some on his chest and a playful Ryan dribbled more onto Mike's boxers. From there, the hangovers had been forgotten.

Ryan slowed down on the dirt road and the car felt the bumps. After twenty minutes, an eyesore broke the ennui of the desert landscape: a battered trailer surrounded by scarred lawn furniture. A fake deer with bleached and broken antlers guarded the door. An old Ford pickup truck, hood flipped open, rested unhitched nearby.

Ryan pulled up beside the trailer. He craned his neck out the open window and called out. "¡Oye ese! ¿Que hay de nuevo?"

Moments later the trailer door popped open. Squinting at the sun from the darkness of the interior, a dusky-skinned, stout man stepped out. His pitch-black hair was pulled back in a ponytail. Shirtless, his chest was a blend of curved muscle and fat around his stomach, a torso in transition from football-player bulk to couch potato.

"Hola."

Ryan grinned at Mike. "Get ready for some of the best shit you'll ever taste," he said as he got out of the car. "Cruz," he called out and met the dealer with a hand slap.

"Baja, you brought a friend." Cruz looked Mike over from top to bottom, while rubbing the scruff along his neck.

"Baja?" Mike worried the two had once played around.

"Heh, I call him that," Cruz said, playfully batting at Ryan's chest. "He's all Californian. So, you have money?"

Ryan pulled a wad of folded bills from a pocket of his cargo shorts. Cruz smiled. "Good. Come inside."

The trailer was dim and much too warm. Mike grimaced at the rank blend of sweat, marijuana smoke, and fried sausage. Cruz led them to the left and back before collapsing on the unmade bed, a stained mattress peeking through tangled sheets, and reaching for shoeboxes scattered along a shelf.

"Mescalito," Cruz said and yawned as he took down one box. Mike glanced inside at the plastic bag filled with what looked like a bunch of dried little turds.

Ryan reached in took out one of the small buttons. "It's the top of a local cactus." He popped it into his mouth then grimaced as he chewed.

Mike did the same. The taste was hot and bitter, leaving his tongue and mouth numb. "Ugh, and to think I'm wasting my time majoring in history."

Ryan smirked. "That shit's tradition to the natives. More than the chupacabra."

"Goat-sucker?" Cruz barked a laugh. "Here, the only thing good for sucking is this." Cruz grabbed the crotch of his cut-offs and squeezed the outline of his cock. Mike doubted the dealer wore any underwear.

Cruz next rummaged and found a fat joint that he lit on the trailer's burner. He took a deep hit, then held it out to Ryan. "*¿Grilla, Baja?*"

"When do I ever say no?" Ryan took several deep hits, refreshing the stink in the air, before passing it to Mike.

The pot was strong, stronger than he'd ever had, though maybe it was 'cause of the peyote button he had just swallowed. His stomach felt queasy. He passed the joint back to Cruz who smirked at both of them.

"I can give you some of this for free...only..."

"Only what?" Mike asked.

"Only *ir a rechinar la cama.*"

Ryan laughed.

"What does that mean?" Mike asked.

Ryan stepped close to his roommate. He slipped his arms around Mike's neck and lightly kissed him, making him blush. "He wants to fuck around."

Mike stared at Cruz, who began unbuttoning his shorts. The trail of dark hair began around his stomach and got thicker the lower it went. "I...I..."

"Don't worry 'bout it, Mikey," Ryan giggled. "I go through this all the time with Cruz. You don't have to join in."

Ryan turned back to Cruz and took the joint from the dealer's mouth. He took one last hit and then passed it to Mike, who watched as his best friend slipped his shorts off.

Mike couldn't stay to watch. He wouldn't. The inside of the trailer felt blistering hot and his head throbbed, like too much blood circulated around his temples. He stumbled outside, trying not to think of them together.

The setting sun was not the right color. It took him a moment staring at the sunset to realize the red had changed to a purplish hue, like the desert at midnight. He stood there, trying not to eavesdrop on the loud springs complaining and the grunts and groans. When he heard Cruz yell out, "*Chupame la polla*," Mike moved further away from the trailer, his eyes never straying from the horizon.

Something moved out there. The rocks maybe. They looked taller, more angular. No, something definitely shifted near the sunset. A shape, scuttling over the desert.

He watched it move until he felt so sick from the colors and the heat in his stomach that he leaned over and vomited on the hard soil. A bit of his lunch stained his sandals and feet.

When he looked back up the nearby ceramic deer seemed ten feet tall and frowned down at him. A little frightened, he looked away. The shape was closer. It must have moved quickly when he wasn't watching. He could make it out now. A hunched-over figure. Maybe. It looked dark against all the colors that had sprung up on the desert. It crawled over the outcroppings, now and then leaping towards him.

Mike watched it twitch and scamper, now some fifty feet off. He could see the failing light shine off large black eyes staring at him. The thing's outline wavered, for a moment shifting to become just a fractal of the landscape's kaleidoscope, before returning. Only this time he could see spines raised along the thing's back.

Damn. Mike shuffled forward, stepping into a ditch and twisting his ankle. It took far too long for the pain to reach his head and make him look down. Each toe had become stretched to amazing proportions. He wiggled them and marveled at how they could go on for miles.

The deer began laughing at him. It had Ryan's voice.

When he glanced up the spiny thing was close. For a moment, its stare shifted to the same green hue as his roommate's eyes. From its slack mouth unfurled a long tongue. Instinctively, Mike leaned in closer.

The very end of the imagined—he knew it had to be imagined—chupacabra's tongue lifted towards his face. The puckered tip had a glistening dew drop. Mike half-closed his eyes and licked his lips remembering that kiss with Ryan. It had been smoky, tickling the back of his throat, and not fading as the drug flowed through his lungs. Mike had never wanted it to end, but it had. He hoped this new kiss, however how delusional, promised more than his first.

AUTHOR'S NOTE

IN HIGH SCHOOL, I'd waited months to sleep over at Scott Blanche's house.

We'd known each other for years, back before he became one of the most popular boys around and before I'd completely sunk into the woodwork. We played games together. He had a beautiful, heart-shaped face like a barn owl.

I'd come to think of Scott's bedroom as some mystery that needed solving. The brief glimpses I'd had of it when I came over his house enticed me: a battered kettledrum as a table, cassette tapes leaking shiny black strands on the carpet, and a bed with tousled sheets and no pillows.

Mysteries demand questions. And foremost in my mind was what did Scott wear to bed? I imagined him lying in only his white briefs. As I changed in the bathroom down the hall, I looked at the pajamas I'd brought. Flannel, a candy-apple red. I could not be more embarrassed by wearing them if they had vinyl-coated feet. But I could not bring myself to walk into his room practically naked.

He was already in bed when I came back. Sure enough, he was bare-chested, the comforter teasing me where it lay just above his flat stomach. He told me to close the door. Scott's new puppy, ugly and hairless, missing some teeth too, was curled at his feet. He'd told me his mother had brought it back from a recent trip to Mexico.

I slipped into the sleeping bag on the floor beside the bed.

He reached over and turned on his clock radio. "I can't sleep without noise," he said. When he turned off the light, the green glow of the radio made his exposed skin radioactive.

We talked about nothing, the way you can do when you're fifteen and everything seems at once boring and maddening. I was in the midst of telling him my adventures in Amelia Island, Florida, half of which were lies I hoped would impress, when I realized he wasn't listening but staring at the door. I noticed the hall light through the bottom crack turn on and off. His mother going to bed.

Scott smiled as he got out of bed. Though much of the room was dark, my eyes had adjusted. I stared as he walked over to his dresser. The white briefs made his ass glow like a will-o'-the-wisp.

He took care pulling the top draw completely free. He ripped something taped to the back. His hands were full when he returned. "Ever smoke pot?"

I'd never seen anyone roll a joint before. My heart raced.

Familial piety and guilt had kept me from the more fun sins. Despite knowing where my folks kept the keys to the liquor cabinet, I'd never stolen a drink when they were away. Instead, I'd scurry up the bookshelf, find the key in the dust of the topmost shelf, then pull out the bottles, uncork some and sniff, wondering what they might taste like. But then I always put them back as I'd found them. I'd never kissed anyone, girl or guy, yet, though I ached to do so. And I'd never once thought about trying drugs.

As I watched him light the twisted joint, the orange glow from the lighter's flame at odds with the clock radio's emerald aura, I realized how scared I was at witnessing something so alien.

He breathed in the smoke before offering the joint to me. Words rushed out of my mouth on a current of anxiety. "I-I'm asthmatic. It would kill me. Poison to my weak lungs." I held up my inhaler as proof. Scott laughed and wisps leaked from his mouth. My face burned.

He patted the bed at his lap, and for a moment, I was stunned by the invitation to climb into bed and sit on him. But then I realized he'd called for the puppy, which came over with an eager wag. He took a deep drag and blew smoke in the puppy's face. "Cheech likes it," he said and chuckled.

The puppy licked his face. I wondered if Scott would let me do the same if I smoked the joint. I almost asked him to hand it over.

He shared more smoke with the puppy, then lay back down and closed his eyes. I yammered on and on, barely above a whisper. How the caterpillar in Alice in Wonderland smoked a hookah. How many times I'd seen Disney's version of Peter Pan. How the puppy's slate-gray skin felt like velour. No, like Naugahyde. Naugahyde. Not like the soft fur of my cat.

Scott had fallen asleep.

Back then, my fantasies had been organized in a complex and pyramidal hierarchy. Every boy at school had his place, with Scott at the very summit. Most nights, I imagined myself as a vampire, using hypnotism to make them want me. Now and then I'd sip their blood, but the thought of bringing my lips to their neck or chest was more exciting than drinking.

For the past two years, I'd not reached the higher tiers of that pyramid. Not legitimately. There were just too many boys, and I loved telling myself the same story, over and over again: a slow seduction that made it difficult to finish with the lesser let alone attain the betters.

But after a night's gaming with Scott, I always cheated and made the fast ascent. The stories I conceived as I ground my hips into the mattress were never about us having sex. No, I imagined him beneath one of the girls that stared at him openly at school.

I jerked off while he slept inches away, then used my inhaler.

SOUNDS COMING FROM somewhere in the house woke me. Scott remained in bed, though the sheets had been kicked down to his shins. How many had seen him like this? I wanted to stroke his skin, but more noise distracted me. His bedroom door was open. I crept into the hall. The noise, a whimpering, came from the kitchen.

His puppy sat in front of the open fridge with its paws on the lowest shelf. It turned its head to me. Black pebble eyes reflected the light from the fridge. "Make me a thandwich." Its missing teeth and lolling tongue gave it a bad lisp. "I have the munchieth. Thath what happenth."

I took several steps back, almost tripped and fell.

It tried wagging its tail. "Do you thee the crap they feed me?"

I sat down. My pajamas confined the coldness of the linoleum to my hands and feet. The puppy had to know all his owner's secrets. "Teach me a trick with Scott."

The puppy sneezed. Or maybe snorted. "Let me gueth. Cat perthon." It stuck its head into the fridge and I heard plastic wrap being torn.

I went back to Scott's bedroom. I tangled one foot in the unreeled cassettes and pressed one hand down on the mattress for balance as I freed myself. He didn't stir. The lighter was by his bare shoulder. I considered taking it as a memento of that night, but theft seemed something more apt for a dog person. Dogs would only steal things so as to bury them.

Scott's lips parted slightly and a bit of smoke slipped free. It disappeared before I could catch it and mend my regret at not sharing that joint with him, missing the taste of his saliva.

I remember climbing into his bed. How could any dream be so clear after all these years, unless it wasn't a dream?

I straddled him.

Cats are sneaky and steal babies' breath. I'd always wondered why they'd want to. I leaned in so my lips brushed against his—so soft, so soft—and inhaled. The tip of my tongue slid across his teeth, his inner cheek, swept into my mouth whatever clues to his life I could. I savored years of smoke and the sweetness of his charm.

That was my first kiss.

ALWAYS LISTEN TO A GOOD PAIR OF UNDERWEAR

STEVE LIKED LATE mornings best. That was when his roommate Mike would crawl out of bed and make his way, first to bathroom, then to kitchen, and finally into the den and slump down on the sofa with a glass of orange juice. Still sleepy, the corners of his brown eyes crusty and heavy, he would wipe his face like a child, the gesture overdone.

Steve liked late mornings best because Mike slept in the most wondrous boxers imaginable. They had to be magic.

Steve kept glancing back and forth, from the television set to the zone of Mike's waist, a flat stomach slightly decorated with a trail of curly hair, thick legs, and, in between, white boxers studded with full red lips.

Mike stretched and yawned, oblivious to Steve's gaze. The fly of his boxers stretched wide, allowing a glimpse of something pink and fleshy and wonderful. The mouths on the boxers smirked and a dozen tongues licked those lips. One near the waistband smacked noisily.

Yesterday, Steve had marveled at the school of goldfish that swam around Mike's thighs and almost off the cotton onto the sofa. Another morning, letters spelled out WANT ME WANT ME WANT like a digital marquee from Times Square on his roommate's ass.

Steve did the laundry; hell, did pretty much all the housework. Italian men liked their mates subservient, Mike always joked, and knowing that he shared the two-bedroom flat with a gay guy seemed to cast Steve in the role of the little woman. When he lifted out the magic boxers from the clothes hamper, they were a dead white, often still warm from Mike's body. Before he hand-washed them in the sink, he would bring them to his face, sniffing once and smiling if he caught sight of any small, curly hairs left in the crotch. He once nibbled on one, but it had no taste.

So what if I'm insane, Steve thought, *at least I'm in love*. He had written to the twink behind a help column on a gay youth site, admitting his crush on his roommate, how every day he was mesmerized by Mike's boxers, and signed it with his real name (he never cared for the corny noms-des-plumes like Lost in Love or Smeared Second that people used). The peroxide addict responded with a suggestion that Steve start taking Thorazine.

"Psst," whispered one of the mouths on Mike's underwear. "Psst."

Steve turned from the commercial promising all the flavor of beef in an aerosol spray to make your vegetables taste like they were grown at a Texas ranch. Mike had fallen back asleep, his head supported by one muscular arm. Autumn sunlight from the window turned his skin to bronze.

"C'mere. Come closer." The voice was low and breathless.

"Aww, he's a shy one," another mouth muttered. "Loser."

Steve knew he should be getting to class. But without really meaning to, he inched closer to Mike on the sofa.

"That's it." One of the mouths talked like a tipsy drag queen. "Just move on over an' get some of what you been aching for." A cloth tongue pulled at the edges of the fly, allowing more of Mike's cock to be seen.

Steve felt his own mouth grow dry. He envied all the spit the mouths on Mike's magic boxers must have. Some even drooled.

"He knows you snort his shorts."

Several of them giggled like schoolgirls.

"Mmmmhmmm. Boy's got it bad for this one."

"Doesn't know what's what, what is, and what could be."

Steve didn't like being razzed. Not by the kids back in high school, not by the old fart with the bad hairpiece at his last summer job, and certainly not by underwear, no matter how sexy. He started to get up.

"Now don't be running off so fast."

"We have something to show you."

The mouths began licking Mike's dick, which responded to the massage by growing larger and larger.

"Oooh, look at that."

"Seven—"

"Shit, that's eight if I ever saw it." The mouth kissed the reddish tip which began to leak sticky fluid. "Sweet sap too."

Steve stood there, his own crotch suddenly active and feeling a little constrained. He wanted nothing more than to unzip and begin playing. The only thing that stopped him was pure envy, along with the notion that he needed to buy his underwear from some place other than K-mart.

Why were they being such a tease? What possibly could a pair of boxers want, Steve wondered. *A lavender sachet in the drawer? Just brushing Mike's skin should have been enough. Maybe they had grown greedy? Or rebellious?*

"We're lonely, babe."

Steve took a step closer. The floorboards under his foot creaked and Mike shifted in his sleep.

"Not for you." One tongue stuck out and gave him a rude raspberry.

"We want a mate." A chorus of "mate" followed for several seconds.

Steve scratched his head. "So, umm, like you want me to buy him another pair? A thong?" Mike's stiff penis momentarily bobbed, distracting him.

"Think, fool. Aren't we bottoms?"

He shrugged. Honestly, he had never given it much thought, though it did make sense.

"Shit, you think Miss Thing would know another of her kind."

"Loser."

"Now listen here," said the mouth that had been lucky enough to give Mike the most intimate of kisses. Its lips still gleamed with pre-cum.

Steve could not believe what he was hearing. He shook his head after a moment. "No way, his chest is my favorite part." Indeed it was, the perfect map with typography of smooth skin, taut layers of firm muscle over bone.

"Then guess you'll never be seeing *this* again." The mouths began pinching at the fly as Mike's penis, abandoned of attention, began to wilt.

"Wait," Steve hissed. He could not turn back, not after catching sight of something so breathtaking. "Can you do more?"

Several chuckles erupted from the underwear. "Maybe. Treat us right and you'll be in for a treat for yourself."

That was all Steve needed to hear...

=

LATE THE NEXT morning, Mike stumbled into the living room, sipping from a glass of fresh-squeezed. With his free hand he lightly tugged at the shoulder strap of the white, ribbed tank top. Steve had bought it yesterday and had half-expected Mike to take one look at the gift and make some nasty remark but instead he had greeted both present and Steve with a wide grin.

Steve smiled at the tiny red hearts that rose up from the boxers like champagne bubbles, up onto the tank top to pop, exploding in pink fireworks. A larger red heart beat with a disco staccato over the covered spot of Mike's left pectoral.

As Mike passed by him on the sofa, he lifted a hand and roughly yet fondly swept it through Steve's hair. The touch was electric, sending shivers down his body.

All it needed was a good top, Steve thought. *Like me. Love was definitely a magical thing.*

AUTHOR'S NOTE

YES, I HAD a roommate named Mike. Michael Carte.

I met him freshman year at Tulane and latched on to him like a puppy. I became adept at timing my visits to his dorm room when he about to change and he never showed the least hesitance to strip off his clothes or a towel in front of me. I had never been so close to another nude guy. That year, I learned how to stare in quick doses. Italian, he had the mesomorphic grace of a natural athlete. And yes, the perfect chest.

I was an introverted virgin who craved time spent in the presence of someone who had... well, so much presence. Glamour. He could enchant anyone. From sophomore year on, we shared an apartment. He would often walk around clad only in boxers. Even now, I can close my eyes and remember how he would lie on the sofa, as if posing for my benefit alone.

THE HIGH COST OF TAMARIND

IVAN WONDERED WHY Sandro had taken him down to the docks; the only open cinema remaining in Tampico was not near the waterfront. On a late Saturday morning, the docks were quiet except for a few tired gulls, which squawked at the boys in annoyance for not bringing any offerings. Sandro walked slowly down one rickety wooden platform to the edge. Ivan winced at how his best friend—no, Sandro was more than that, they needed a new word for all he meant to him—favored one leg. The one without the sick bone.

Wary of loose boards and rusty nails, Ivan sat down next to Sandro. The air held a terrible smell that made both their eyes tear. Worse than spoiled eggs or meat or milk. Ivan leaned forward. The water beneath them was murky and dark with spilt oil and whatever else the old factories had poured out. Somewhere along the docks, they had passed a sign that warned against swimming. Ivan couldn't imagine anyone crazy enough to let that water touch bare skin. It would seep into the flesh and cause sickness. Maybe turn the bones against the body, as Sandro's had.

"Think they have tamarind candy at the *Regio*?"

Sandro shrugged and began searching the inside pocket of his worn jacket.

Ivan thought he might be looking for a pack of cigarettes. He hated when Sandro smoked. It made the boy's mouth taste awful. "Or maybe they'll have hot chocolate?" Rich and semi-sweet. That would cover any hint of ash on Sandro's tongue.

Sandro held out not a cellophane wrapped package but a tiny red box. The one Ivan had given him at the last *Día de los Reyes*.

"Your ring." Ivan felt his stomach fall out of his torso and land in the stinking water. Did Sandro mean to give it back? Ivan had saved up for months of sweeping the crosswalks in town to afford a band of gold that didn't look brittle.

=

"The President and I have conferred about your proposal. We are interested in supporting the efforts of Germany in return for diplomatic, financial, and military assistance. We shall begin sending troops and munitions north along the border. Should the United States of America enter the war we will reclaim our lost territories. General Villa expressed interest in Zeppelins. Von Kardoff recommends submarine presence at Tampico." Signed, ZAPATA.

A plain textual edition of the Zapata Telegram (1917), as found at the Imperial Prussian Archives in Berlin in 1968.

=

"Chalina saw some news program on the television." Sandro turned the jewelry box over and over. "Showed an American hospital. It was so white and clean."

Ivan had visited Sandro at the Hospital Vera Cruz and remembered how cramped and dingy each room felt.

"Your sister watches so much television she thinks she could speak New York."

"It's empty."

Ivan laughed. "Not as crowded as Mexico City, but empty?"

"No, this box." Sandro placed it on the dock between them. "Maybe. I whispered a prayer into it and tightly shut the lid. Maybe it's still inside."

Ivan reached for both Sandro's hands. All the fingers were bare. How had he not noticed? Sandro always wore his gift when they went to the morning show. The *Regio* was never crowded then and they could sit in the seats and lean against one another and hold hands in the cool darkness.

"What happened? Did your father find it?"

Sandro shook his head. "There's a small shop in town with grimy windows. He buys jewelry without asking questions."

Ivan wiped at his eyes. He blamed the chemicals rising off the water. "Why?"

"I can hitch north to the occupied territories. If I can get to Austin they have vans there that will cross into América."

"We could go to New Orleans maybe?" Ivan had always wanted to go there ever since he heard of Mardi Gras. Soon after Tropsch Petrochemicals GmbH transferred his father from Berlin to Tampico, Ivan's family attended Mass at Saint Boniface. He had first seen Sandro sitting quiet, with his head down. The only reason he went without complaint each week to church was the hopes of seeing the Mexican boy again. After they finally became friends, Ivan had avoided Boniface. New Orleans had grand churches but he wanted to really worship the streets where they laughed and danced. Tampico lacked both.

"No."

"Then New York?"

Sandro gripped Ivan's fingers. "Just me. If you went, they might arrest you. I would not know where you are."

═══

THE ENTRY FOR the Battle of Tampico in the 1963 Zedler Universallexikon:

> *The Battle of Tampico was an engagement of the Great War (Apr., 1914) fought in and around the prosperous port*

town of Tampico. This event served to bring Mexico into the war. In the winter months of 1914, diplomatic relations, the Concordar, developed between the German Empire and Mexico through the efforts of the Foreign Secretary, Arthur Zimmermann, and Emiliano Zapata Salazar, military advisor to President Adolfo de la Huerta.

Imperial undersea boats arrived in early April of 1914 at Tampico and surprised the American fleet, commanded by Admiral Henry T. Mayo, which had settled in the area to protect American petroleum interests. The *Dolphin*, flagship of the American Atlantic Fleet, was among the vessels sunk (though some current historians debate whether sabotage may have been involved). The attack successful, the undersea boats continued to safeguard the Gulf of Mexico. Financed by the Empire, Mexico invaded the bordering American states of Arizona and Texas. By securing the Tamaulipas region, the Empire ensured the success of the Concordar and the explosive growth of the Mexican petroleum industry.

Bibliography: See M. Stürmer, *The Concordar's Role in America's Defeat*. Bertelsmann, 2000.

=

"So you'd leave me so easily?"

"I want to see the insides of their hospitals. They must work miracles. Clean and white miracles."

Ivan nodded. "Fix your bones."

"Then I can come back here."

Ivan wondered why anyone would ever leave such a wondrous place. Did such hospitals find people hiding in the corners, wanting to stay forever? Would a Sandro who could dance on good legs without cancer ever return to the dirt of Tampico?

His first and only love picked up the box and reached back with his arm to throw it into the Gulf.

"Wait." Ivan gently but firmly stopped his arm.

"I want to throw out my prayer. Maybe if it floats out to clean water—"

Ivan pried open Sandro's fingers. The box felt warm, almost sweaty. "I'll keep your prayer." He brought the box, which felt heavy, as if the ring remained still hidden inside, to his lips and kissed the lid once.

=

Protesters Burn Waters and Damage Docks
Marcela Valente

TAMAULIPAS, 5 Apr (MPS) - Residents from the region converged on the small port of Tampico to stage a waterfront rally, protesting the role Petroleos Mexicanos (PEMEX) has in allegedly polluting the Gulf. Wearing carnival masks resembling buzzards and demons, the protestors escalated into violence when police arrived to detain them. Oil poured into the water was set ablaze, generating thick black clouds that could be seen for miles. Official reports estimate that property damages nearing over two million pesos will hamper the recovery of the impoverished district for years.

=

IVAN SPENT A week fashioning the ogre mask, coloring it angry. The time felt nearly as long as the past year without Sandro. Behind the wall of papier-mâché, he could barely see the woman light the gas-soaked rag stuck in the bottle he held. One eyehole was too low. But he could feel the heat.

He rushed down the dock. The sirens chased him, but not yet the police. He felt like a hero from the movies.

Even with the burning bottle spreading acrid smoke, he could still smell the stench of the waters. He knew they had made Sandro's bones turn against him. Like bullets left too long in the body, poisoning a man's blood, the ships war had sent to the bottom had left the Gulf weak, too sick to resist PEMEX's dumping. Ivan's father could tell the long, complicated names of every chemical swirling in the tide. Ivan only cared that they would burn, cauterizing the water. As he tossed the makeshift grenade as far as he could, he hoped the fire would never end.

He felt strong arms grab him. In his last moment of freedom, his other hand opened. The tiny gift-wrapped box fell to the dock. He had whispered to it his own prayer while taping gold paper salvaged from his own *Weihnachten* presents. After a haunting year, Sandro had not returned to him. Ivan managed to kick the box with his foot, so that it would fall into the blaze that erupted. As the officers beat him down, he caught, for only a moment, a smell like perfume—no, more like tamarind candy—rising off the water.

AUTHOR'S NOTE

I REMEMBER ATTENDING *a convention and sitting in the audience for a panel discussing alternate history. I wanted to read stories that presented an alternative England where Oscar Wilde wasn't jailed or an America dealing with James Buchanan's admission that he loved William Rufus King. The panelists seemed content to argue over battles and terminology, while I wondered how many of us retold our own history.*

Would it be better to retell our own histories more to our liking?

Just shy of eighteen, I sold my first story, something silly, to a Midwestern digest. At the time, writing seemed so easy. Words fell upon the page and I needed only care a bit how they were arranged. Nothing prepared me for the forthcoming drought; I didn't sell another piece for a couple years. But knowing that any day that magazine with that first story would show up at my door helped hold back so many disappointments in my life.

I was a sophomore at Tulane when I found the fat package from Kansas City stuffed into our mail slot. I shared the apartment with three other guys, but only Mike mattered to me. The other pair has all but faded from memory.

I remember eagerly tearing open the package. A dozen of Lighthouse Magazine fell into my lap. I'd more than spent my first meager check on additional copies. Lighthouse looked homespun and the script typeface could have come from my mother's Selectric typewriter (which used these cool metal domes covered in raised characters), but I found my byline and, for several minutes, I had a taste of bliss. Until I read the story and discovered the editor had stolen its magic. Literally. Without my permission or even a warning, he'd substituted a filthy king for the villainous wizard.

In my room, I worked through my disappointment by carefully autographing issues with a felt-tipped pen. I struggled to make each cursive letter perfect, as if my penmanship would distract any reader from the story's flaws.

When I handed one to Mike, he didn't even turn a page to read the inscription. That hurt me. But then, Mike would often hurt me.

Later, he wanted to wrestle and pounced on me. I was a scrawny boy of twigs caught in his grasp; he outweighed me by sixty, maybe seventy pounds. When I grew frustrated and started to smack at him to let me go, he became furious and ground my face into the rough carpeting. The skin of my cheek and forehead burned. That eye went dark.

I wondered aloud if I should go to the hospital. He didn't offer to drive me but gave me several aspirin. I was more frightened than resentful. I remember thinking, if I hadn't resisted wrestling, he would never have grown so violent.

My vision cleared in a couple days. Mike acted more bothered by the raw patches on my face that took longer to heal. One night he sat besides me on the second-hand sofa and told me his darkest secret: once at a family gathering, one of his uncles had drank too much and then made a pass at him. That Mike had taken me into such confidence was empowering, yet terrifying. His disgust for the man was clear and vocal. I grew scared that Mike had known my feelings for him, that he'd injured me as a warning.

He went into the kitchen. I heard him puttering around there. Mike rarely did any of the apartment chores. I did them for him. I stayed seated, thinking about the story he'd told me. If it were a fairy tale, even one so simple as what I'd written at seventeen, would the uncle still be the villain? How could anyone resist anyone as strong and handsome as Mike?

Understanding the uncle's weakness, I sat there and rewrote the story in my head and allowed a torrid moment between them. That would have created a precedent, one that offered me hope.

Mike returned with a thermos and two mugs. He poured hot chocolate laced with peppermint schnapps. As he stretched out on the sofa beside me, our legs touched. He did not seem to mind.

I thought to myself, now I'd like to read to Mike my story. Not the one from the magazine, but the story he'd given me. But, I kept quiet as we sipped from our mugs. I never let the happy-ever-after ending loose.

THE PRICE OF
GLAMOUR

These wonders have been lying by your door & mine for ever since we had a door of our own. We had to go a hundred yards off and see for ourselves, but we never did.
　—Thackeray
　London, 1844

Tupp Smatterpit sat on the back of a chestnut-seller's cart, his back warm from resting against the stove. Tupp had sprinkled a pinch of powdered glamour over himself and the old coster driving the wagon believed him to be one of the countless children that roamed Covent Garden's marketplace rather than one of the Folk. As the donkey slowly pulled the cart through the crowd, the gentle sway and the constant tick-tocking of his waistcoat was lulling Tupp to sleep.

He ignored the sounds of vendors calling out their goods and decided to nap a little while. Tupp nudged the back of his bent top hat, once a shiny pearl gray and now dingy as ash, so that it covered not only the tight curls of red hair but also his eyes. A chiming sound came from one of the many pockets of his vest. He groaned at being disturbed and pulled out the right watch for the crime.

The sweeping hands on the enchanted dial not only showed him he had ten minutes to traverse the West End of London but also that the Dowagers, a pair of crones, were nearly through with a robbery.

If Tupp was late in meeting them, a rival bagman might collect the stolen goods. There were other fences in the city besides Tupp's employer, but none as mean spirited as Bluebottle. He was a spriggan, one of the worst of the fey, all bloated with spite and bile.

Tupp didn't dare waste another moment and leapt down from the cart, nearly knocking over a woman with a basket of fresh flowers.

Slightly out of breath after dashing through side streets and avenues, Tupp arrived near Hyde Park with time to spare. The watch stopped chiming a moment later, one of the slender hands pointing where to go next.

In the shadows of the alley, the Dowagers towered over a child shivering and huddled against the brick wall. They were an ancient pair and no one remembered their names. One's eyes were clear, her sister's blind and covered with a gray film. Otherwise they looked identical, tall and thin, almost brittle looking, with fingers that resembled twigs. Their long hair was touched with silver, and they had never abandoned their sackcloth clothing for anything contemporary like so many of the fey who dwelt in London.

The clear-eyed sister, clutching an armful of pretty new clothes to her chest, snatched the bonnet from the head of the girl. The Dowagers, glamoured to resemble rosy-cheeked maids, lured children from the street with promises of sweets only to strip them of everything of worth.

The blind one leaned down and tapped the girl on the forehead twice. "Leave us, child. Vex us not. We have taken enough."

"Enough," hissed her sister.

As the child ran past him, still crying, Tupp nodded to the Dowagers and tipped his hat. "Ladies." He held up his sack, the mark of a bagman's trade.

"A frock, a bonnet, a petticoat." The first Dowager unceremoniously dropped the clothes into the bag. Her blind sister held up a glowing coin the size of a penny. "Stolen laughter. Bluebottle will pay well for a child's humor, no?"

"Five bags of glamour," hissed her blind sister.

"No doubt, m'lady. No doubt." He watched as she dropped the glittering piece after the fine clothes.

Tupp reached into the bag and pulled out a wine bottle and drew the cork. The smell of the cumin lacing the wine filled the air. The Dowagers drew closer, their hands out, fingers curling and curling. Centuries might have passed since they plagued the children of the Celts, only appeased by such a spiced drink, yet their thirst remained.

"It's been so long, Sister," the blind one whispered, the pale worm of a tongue wriggling over her lips.

"Give us the bottle." The other sister's fingernails swept close to his face.

Tupp smiled kindly. "Oh, I shall, I shall. But I'm of a mind for that bit of laugh you threw in. Bluebottle will give you glamour enough for the finery." He let the bottle come close to their hands. "Agreed?"

As he had guessed, they did not hesitate. "Yes," they groaned and the blind one took the bottle and drank deeply, her lips becoming stained with the wine. Her sister did not wait long before grabbing the bottle.

Humming a merry tune as he left them, Tupp withdrew the laughter from the sack and slipped it into one of the pockets of his waistcoat. That bauble was worth a hundred petticoats.

====

THE MAGIC CHARM Tupp had spoken before heading into the sewers had nearly faded and the mire he stood on was beginning to stick to his shoes. But damn Cagmag would not stop digging through the surrounding filth long enough to say anything more than a few words at once. The slimy troll would tower over most fey if it ever stood upright, but down in the tunnels it could move about only on all fours. Cagmag dipped its hooked hands deep into the muck, and then leaned forward to bring a nose that resembled a notched dagger low to sniff around. Tupp was about to depart when the sewer-hunter pulled out a reeking handful and sighed majestically.

"What is it? A copper pot? A candlestick?"

"Pigsty sweepings." The troll opened his black-lipped maw and took a healthy bite of the muck.

Tupp reached for the robbery watch and checked the crime. Nothing. He tapped the dial lightly. The hands still clearly indicated that something of worth was down there, seized by Cagmag.

"Ahh, here's a right bit." The troll lifted out more from the filth. Its lamp-like yellow eyes narrowed a moment. "Had to hide it, there's thieves about."

Tupp leaned in closer, but the mass Cagmag had pulled up looked no better than the sweepings. "Of course there's thieves."

"This one's too bold." The troll's dark tongue licked to reveal a fine riding boot. "Heard a leprechaun complaining some of his goods were stolen from his shop."

Tupp stifled a chuckle. Leprechauns were crooked cobblers and deserved a bit of hardship. More than likely, a customer they cheated was having a bit of satisfaction.

The troll finished cleaning off the boot and held it out to Tupp. "You stole that?"

"Aye." Cagmag tipped it back. "Oh, sorry, there's still a bit of foot left in it. Anxious, I was."

=

By sunset, Tupp was weary from collecting all over London. He arrived late to his next appointment and looked around the emptying marketplace, trying to spot the card sharp the "cheats" watch had led him to. He roamed the area to no avail. Desperate, he ventured into a nearby gin parlor.

Gas lamps that reflected off mirrored panes of glass brightly lit the crowded establishment. Tupp did his best not to be jostled as he took a winding path through the room. Beside a flavored liquor stand, he spotted the shabbily-dressed hobgoblin with his mouse-like whiskers and tufted tail.

The hobgoblin, when he was sober, was skilled at broading, changing the faces of cards with a little bit of magic to cheat unsuspecting men. The faery rapped on the bar to get the server's attention. "Another Celebrated Butter, my good man."

Tupp put a hand over the aromatic dram as the hobgoblin raised it to his wet lips. "Not thinking of drinking away all the pence are you, Rob—"

"Mr. Hobbes to you, sir." The hobgoblin nervously glanced around at the surrounding humans. His long whiskers had been oiled and curled at the tips to resemble a man's mustache. "At least, amid this company."

"Fine, then. There's the matter of your debt. Or shall I tell Bluebottle there's to be no payment?"

Hobbes blanched at the thought and licked his lips. "Oh, no, not that. I nearly earned enough to pay what I owes. You have to put in a good word for me, Tupp. Tell Bluebottle that without more glamour, I'd have to leave London." The hobgoblin moved the glass from underneath Tupp's palm, careful not to spill a drop. "Come now, a dry swallow's a bad thin', we all knows." He rubbed his throat as if parched.

Tupp could see that Hobbes was nearly drunk. Another few shots and his face would turn bluish and he'd pass out. "Where's the day's take?"

"On me person. It's not safe to hide anythin' anymore."

It took Tupp a moment to realize what Hobbes alluded to. "The mysterious thief? Not you, too."

"It's no tall tale. Quite a few of the folk been robbed. Happened to that little portune that's been a-thievin' carriages. And Jenny Greenteeth had brought in quite a haul from a body she...well, she said she found on the banks of the Thames. Kept it all in a cubbyhole by the docks but when Jenny went for it, was gone. Now who'd be so daft as to upset ol' Jenny?"

Tupp felt bad for any fey foolish enough to steal from Jenny, one of the more mean spirited of the Folk. The thief must be a shire pixie, new to the city, and ignorant of whom not to cross. It hadn't been so long since Tupp himself had come from Wessex, seeking his fortune in the grand chaos that was London. He hadn't been any wiser and was still paying the price.

The memory bothered him, making him anxious. He was tempted to buy a drink himself. "Enough of such talk." He held up his sack. "The coin."

Hobbes nodded and shook his right arm a moment before leaning in close and letting it drop over the mouth of the sack. Pence and groats and shillings tumbled out of Hobbes' sleeve. The hobgoblin's sharp fingers snatched the last coin, a guinea, before it fell.

"I'll be needin' this to stay warm tonight."

=

SACK HEAVY WITH the day's haul, Tupp knew he should be heading to Bluebottle's, but made his way to the Royal Exchange, an immense stone building central to human commerce. The small shops along the front, little more than enclosed stands that offered books or newspapers or stationery, were closing for the night. Only a few people walked the Exchange's halls and if they bothered to notice Tupp, thanks to a pinch of glamour he'd seem nothing more than a lost youth.

On the upper floor of the northern side of the building was a coffeehouse, nearly deserted at that late hour. He moved to the back and opened the door of a storeroom. Tupp easily climbed over the aromatic sacks of beans to reach a forgotten trapdoor in the ceiling that led to a small attic and his home.

A man would have to stoop, but being just four feet tall, Tupp needed only to worry about his hat being knocked off his head. At the far end of the room was a mound of goose feathers that served as a bed. As tempting as it was to relax a while, he could not afford the luxury at the moment.

He moved to the wall, his fingers finding and pulling free the loose stone. In the niche was a mound of treasure, the cream secretly skimmed from the milk of Tupp's tasks over the past years. He reached into his waistcoat pocket, found the laughter he had bartered from the Dowagers and added it to the pile.

Bluebottle, that artless plume-plucked maggot-pie, would be surprised at such a lovely hoard. Tupp was especially proud of the mourning brooch containing a lock of hair from a woman with the Sight. Took quite a bit of trickery to wrest the brooch from a dreary Irish ankou. What with all that wearing black and a gaunt face pinched like eating something sour, no wonder the bloke had found work as a professional mourner.

Tupp's mind was often nimbler than his fingers. Yet he was not so crafty as to have escaped servitude. He regretted again, for the thousandth time, being so impetuous when he first came to London.

He had been told there was but one source for good quality glamour, the fine powder that enabled any fey to disguise itself to humans without the Sight, a necessity to survive in London. All the iron the humans used to build and live in the city eroded a fey's natural ability. Tupp, new to the city, lacked the coin or the goods to buy from Bluebottle, so there was only one recourse. He had thought himself up to the task, sneaking into the second-hand shop after nightfall and exploring the back rooms, only to be easily caught by the spriggan. Tupp was lifted up by his shirt collar and saw that cages with frightened pixies hung from the rafters. Bluebottle would have dropped him into a massive grinder with rusty gears and teeth and made glamour out of him, if Tupp hadn't been quick with his words. He begged and flattered, promising whatever services the spriggan desired. Bluebottle listened and made the little fey swear to serve as his bagsman for twelve years, one for every of Tupp's fingers that tried to steal from him.

He wondered how long before this thief would make the same mistake.

===

As he walked down the dingiest alley in all of creation, nearer and nearer to Bluebottle's rag-and-bottle shop, Tupp's mood darkened. The door was two planks of wood nailed together and the outside had been painted a jaundiced yellow so that even the oldest and simplest scavengers could find the shop. Bluebottle traded glamour for stolen goods that he would sell back to humans. Nearly every fey in the city owed him, some far worse than others.

Tupp walked in to find Bluebottle mending the frame of a wooden cage. The spriggan had a squat, almost lumpy body. His scruffy jowls and bald pate almost made him resemble a man, but the eyes were different, too small and shiny.

"Ah, my little coney's back." Bluebottle's voice had a rasp, one almost painful to hear.

Tupp swallowed his rage at the insult. He hefted up the sack onto the counter. "A fine haul today."

Bluebottle narrowed his eyes. "We'll see." The spriggan put down the cage and snapped his fingers. To his right on the counter rested an immense ledger. The book opened and the pages flipped on their own.

Tupp emptied the sack and Bluebottle began rummaging. He picked up a tin of tobacco and shook it near his small ear.

"One tin of Byer's Aromatic Cherry Tobacco. Full but dented along one side."

"From the glaistig," Tupp mentioned.

Along the pages of the ledger ink blossomed, adding in the entry. A faint whisper of "Seven pence," rose from the leather binding.

The spriggan reached for the young girl's clothes. "The Dowagers?" Tupp nodded. "One bonnet. One frock. One petticoat, the latter with slight tear along the shoulder."

"Six shillings," said the magic ledger.

"That's not even a bag of glamour's worth."

Bluebottle shrugged.

Tupp swallowed his worry that they'd dare tell the spriggan about his private deal with them for the laughter. He rattled off the names of the other fey who had stolen the goods he brought. Then he grabbed his sack and headed for the door, but was pulled back by a hand at his collar.

"A moment." Bluebottle tapped the pages of the ledger. "You filled your snuff box the other day with glamour, my coney. Are you paying for it now or shall your debt to me grow greater?"

Tupp became flushed but kept his voice calm. "All I have left is tuppence. You shaved my earnings down to a few pence."

The soft voice of the book spoke. "Tupp Smatterpit. Owing eighty-one pounds to date."

"Heh, might as well be your weight in gold. You'll always be bound to me."

"Not true," Tupp chirped.

"Oh?" The spriggan leaned over the counter. His breath was rank. "I'd free you from your service this very moment if you paid your tally."

Tupp left the shop with Bluebottle's coarse laughter at his back. He ran all the way to the Exchange, giddy with the notion that, thanks to his hoard and the spriggan's ignorance, he'd soon be free. But there he found the stone that hid his cache had already been moved. The niche was empty, completely gone.

Tupp choked back a sob. All his work, all his savings over the years, all gone. He'd be working for that artless clotpole forever.

In a lumpish daze, Tupp wandered until he fell into a small crowd watching a street musician playing folk tunes on his hurdy-gurdy. Nearby, a young girl sold seedcakes from a basket. Tupp found a halfpenny in his pocket, his last remaining coin, and bought one of the treats, nibbling it quickly and not leaving a single crumb on his fingerless mittens.

One of the watches began to chime, and he was tempted to throw it across the street. Why hadn't it rung for him? Every theft by a fey should ring the magic watches. Out of instinct he looked at the dial, barely caring that a tiny boggan was picking pockets. It had only been a couple of hours since he had left for Bluebottle's. There might still be time to catch the thief and recover his goods. He needed help, though, and there was only one of the Folk with the necessary gift.

=

TUPP KNEW THAT the rook girl had an appetite for glamour. Though not truly a thief, she needed to cover up her bird feet if she wanted to charm men into buying her drinks and meals. He had been searching for her for over an hour, dashing through the better parts of London. He finally found her gazing at herself in the reflection of a jeweler's window. Her long black tresses flowed from beneath a dark, feathered hat that had seen better days.

She looked down at him with a sad smile. "I've nothing for your master, little one." As if to prove her poverty, she lifted up her hem to show not stockinged feet but scaly claws.

Tupp reached into a pocket and withdrew his snuffbox. He opened the lid and showed her the glittering dust within. "Nearly full." Her eyes went wide and he snapped the lid shut. "Perhaps a trade is in order?"

A few moments later, her dark children, the ravens that spent their days at the Tower of London, were settling on his shoulders. Their eyes were the sharpest in the city and little escaped their notice. With raw cackles they told him the one he wanted was down on Cutler Street in the seedy neighborhood of Houndsditch.

=

WHEN TUPP ROUNDED the corner onto Cutler, the only figure on the street was leaving a dilapidated building. Tupp might have ignored the fellow, who seemed almost lost underneath a heavy coat, had he not flipped up a shining coin—easily recognizable as the stolen laughter—into the air a moment before catching it in his palm.

"You there," Tupp called out.

The figure turned, a face going pale with fear. Then the thief ran, not down the street, but back into the hovel. Tupp followed only a few steps behind him.

Inside was dank and smoky. The thief dashed up a rickety flight of stairs that groaned even under Tupp's light weight. He passed open doorways of rooms with people crowded around tables with cards or throwing dice. On the next floor there were cries as the humans wagered on a pair of burly men boxing in a corner. Tupp stifled his curiosity to look further and continued chasing his quarry.

Ahead of him, the thief threw open a trapdoor to the rooftop. Tupp was almost nipping at his heels. Overhead, the London night sky was clouded from belching chimneys. The thief soon neared the edge of the roof but did not stop or slow and soon was nearing the edge. With a mad leap, arms swinging, he covered the gap to the nearest building. Tupp easily jumped after him. The thief tripped on his coat and fell onto his side. Tupp landed right on the rogue's back bearing him to the ground.

"Quite a chase," said Tupp, trying to catch his breath. "But now there's the matter of what is mine."

When Tupp turned the thief over, he expected to see the slender features of an elf or a scraggly brown-furred boggart, not the face of a scared sixteen-year-old human boy. The faery drew back in shock.

A child, a human child! How could this be? Tupp's mind whirled but he could not disbelieve. It made sense, when he thought about it, explaining why his watches had never chimed at any of the thefts.

The boy glared at Tupp.

"So what are you, the seventh son of a seventh son?" Tupp placed a foot on the boy's chest, keeping him down for the moment. "Have a water-bored stone?"

"What are you talking about?"

"What gives you the Sight?"

The lad gave an embarrassed smile. "Was only a bit of soot in me eyes. Back a few years I worked as a climbing boy. Served a right foul-mouthed sweep, I did, who'd threaten to burn me feet if I didn't climb chimneys fast." The boy shook his head ruefully. "One day found me in this tight bit. Something crawled above me but weren't a rat. You'd think that, well...maybe not you, sir. As it left, it dropped some soot on me face and as I blinked me eyes I saw a li'l fellow scrambling out the top. Ever since then, I see things."

Brownies, Tupp knew, lurk in chimneys on cold mornings. Troublesome little ones that keep to houses. A scattering of ash from the heel in the eye was as good as any faery ointment.

Tupp looked over the boy. He was thin, almost swallowed up by the overcoat. His hair was dark and his eyes were green like wild clover. A bit cleaned up and he'd be handsome enough for a plaything. "Do you have a name?"

"Lind."

"Right then." Tupp offered a hand. The youth cautiously took it and stood up.

"So, what now? You're not going to be cursing me?"

"Now there's the problem. If it were known that a human had robbed the Folk..." Tupp grimaced at the thought. "Well, more than a few of your kind would find themselves at a horrid end." Tupp removed his hat and scratched at his head. "If you return the things you stole from me, I'd be of a mind to let you go and keep this our little secret."

"If I could, sir, I would. Honest. But everything's sold or lost to cards. Could barely keep this coat and the bauble." He pulled out the shining penny. "Seemed so pretty I didn't have the heart to bet it."

Tupp took the laughter from the boy's hand. "All that's left?" He choked out the words. It would take him years to amass enough again to buy his freedom. He was doomed to serve Bluebottle forever, running around sewers with trolls, consorting with the dregs of the city.

He turned to Lind. "You spleeny reeling-ripe fool! I wouldn't worry about magistrates after we get through with you. Dancing till your feet bleed. Making your belly swell, your eyes pop." He poked the boy in the stomach.

"No, sir. Please, sir, a few days and I'll repay everything. I'm a fine cracksman, a master burglar." Lind said and puffed out his thin chest. "Ask any around Houndsditch or Whitechapel. There's not a house I can't break into. A few nights' work is all I need."

Tupp considered a moment. He lacked the power to do more than annoy the boy for the rest of his days. He was surprised that Lind was offering to make amends; he had always thought humans a rather dull, cowardly lot. Perhaps not all were so bad. "A fine cracksman?"

Lind grinned. "Aye. None better."

The boy's bravado amused Tupp. He must have a good measure of skill to have pulled off the thefts. Perhaps there was a way. Bluebottle had to have a small fortune in coin after selling all the stolen goods to the humans. It would be fitting revenge to have the boy break in, swipe enough coin to pay off his debt, and then be free of service before the spriggan even realized the theft!

"If you do wish to make amends, meet me here tomorrow night."

Lind nodded and grabbed hold of Tupp's hand, shaking it. "Thank you, sir. I won't be late."

Tupp watched as the boy ran off. He told himself not to worry that he was putting so much faith on one who wasn't even his own.

=

Tupp knew that every night, well past midnight, Bluebottle dined at the dust-yards, where the city's dust and refuse was heaped and sifted for valuables. The spriggan would devour great handfuls of grit and grime.

So late the following evening, he led Lind to the closed rag-and-bottle-shop.

"We're not going through the front door are we?"

"No. Did that years ago. It's warded—alarmed—and brings Bluebottle fast." Tupp walked around to the side of the building. The wall facing them was crumbling brick and looked dangerous to climb. Old, closed shutters near the slanted roof blocked the only opening other than the front door.

The youth unbuttoned his great coat and withdrew his jemmy, the short crowbar made infamous by burglars. He gave the iron rod a bit of a playful spin in his hand. "An easy job."

"Maybe so. Until we're caught and ground to dust."

Lind's face grew serious. He slipped out of the coat. Beneath, he wore only a threadbare linen shirt and trousers. He thrust the jemmy into a back pocket and rubbed his hands together a moment for warmth before moving to the wall and finding a grip in the loose mortar above his head.

Tupp watched Lind climb and admired the dexterity of the boy. Even when one of Lind's hands misjudged a crack and slipped, he remained quiet and recovered in an instant, swinging his weight onto his other side. Soon he was next to the shutters and carefully prying them open.

In the shadows, Tupp leaned back against the wall and kept his eye on the street. While he waited, he idly considered how he would spend his new freedom. He might become a messenger or perhaps a guide to fey new to the city.

Then he heard the sound of muttering. He peered out from under the brim of his hat to see off in the distance an ungainly shape approaching. His ears caught the word "Hogs," being mentioned again and again.

Tupp realized then that sometimes pigs are let loose at the dust-yards to feed on anything edible. Bluebottle's meal must have been well-picked over by the hogs and he was returning home hungry and cranky.

Tupp doubted Lind had enough time to loot the dark shop. He was torn by the urge to run and leave the boy to his fate—one well deserved, he told himself, after all, he did rob the Folk—and the urge to rescue him. The boy had been true to his word so far and that could not be forgotten. As he started to climb the wall, Tupp swore to himself that he should never ever have thought life in London among the humans would be thrilling.

He easily passed through the small window and, though he fell over ten feet, Tupp landed like a cat on a thick table in the backroom. The inside of the shop was pitch black. He whispered out to Lind and heard a quiet answer next to him.

"Hurry, Bluebottle's returned." Even as he said it, Tupp heard the sound of a key turning in door's heavy lock.

"I haven't found a penny yet," came a whisper back.

"Damn," Tupp said under his breath. His eyes had begun to adjust to the darkness and he got down from the table and found himself next to Lind. "Stay absolutely still."

The floorboards creaked as the spriggan moved through the shop and a nearby door opened as Bluebottle entered the cavernous backroom. He shuffled over to the far corner, at one point passing within inches of the pair, and laid himself down on a bed built into the wall. On a shelf near the spriggan's head was a familiar chest from which Bluebottle paid out Tupp his pitiful earnings.

They waited, holding their breath, as Bluebottle shifted about on the bed, finally becoming still and loosing the occasional snore. Tupp motioned towards the chest. Besides him Lind nodded but then went in the opposite direction, rooting quietly through the spriggan's personal effects.

Tupp could not decide on a fitting curse for the boy as he got down from the table. He crept towards the shelf, pausing twice when Bluebottle shifted about in his sleep. Finally, he stood up on his toes to reach the shelf. As soon as his fingers touched the coffer, the robbery watch in his waistcoat pocket began to chime.

Bluebottle woke in an instant. Tupp was grabbed roughly before he had a chance to flee and shaken about so that the main watchchains he wore jingled.

"A thief! My little coney never learned." Bluebottle brought his face close to Tupp's. The spriggan's mouth opened wide, revealing many rows of dust- and grime-covered teeth. "So which grinder will it be?" He snapped his jaws in anticipation.

Tupp closed his eyes, ready for the end, when all of a sudden

Bluebottle was howling into the little fey's ear. He dared a look and saw the spriggan screaming in pain and, behind him, Lind stabbing at Bluebottle's foot again with the iron jemmy.

Tupp was dropped and, as soon as his feet met the floor, Lind grabbed and pushed him towards a small door. The boy followed, shutting the door behind them and jamming the crowbar into the frame. The wood rattled as Bluebottle pounded away.

The smaller room was faintly lit from the glow of cages hanging from the ceiling beams. There were no other exits; they were trapped. Tupp remembered now where he was: the spriggan's glamour larder.

The imprisoned pixies, all no taller than Lind's forearm even with their glittery wings, were woken by the noise. Thin, sad faces peered out between the bars. A few weak hands stretched out in silent plea.

Tupp looked over at Lind, who held his chest tightly, as if hurt. "Are you all right?'

Lind gave a grin, the sort only a half-crazed fool who craved excitement wore.

"Good." Tupp moved the table with the grinder beneath the nearest cage. "When I give the word, you'll let him in."

The boy looked a bit perplexed, but nodded.

Tupp worked as fast as he could, always mindful of the curses and shouts of his former employer. Finally, he was done, and called out to Lind, who tore loose the jemmy and jumped back.

Bluebottle would have charged into the room if not for the wave of flying pixies that swarmed over him. His angry cries quickly changed to ones of shock and then screams of pain as the freed fey bit at his jowls, ripped his ears, and poked his eyes. Bluebottle collapsed backwards and Tupp and Lind jumped over him. The pixies continued to swarm over the spriggan and their fingers were quickly stained crimson.

Off in the distance came the sounds of a whistle.

"The night watch," said the boy, tugging at Tupp's arm. "A constable heard the screams."

Together they climbed back out of the shop, though the boy seemed oddly labored. Once they dropped down to the alley beside the shop, they fled. Tupp led Lind through the twisted lanes of a slum the Folk knew well. They ended up at a small pub.

Tupp took his seat at an empty table near the fireplace and lifted up two fingers. The serving girl nodded.

Lind looked around nervously. The other patrons were noticeably different from most Londoners. Some had slender ears ending in points, or noses longer than their drinking glasses, or delicate cricket wings that flapped in time to the fiddler playing near the fire.

The boy shivered, still clutching his chest. "So now what?"

Tupp thanked the gal who brought the drinks and caught Lind staring at her back, which was hollow like a serving bowl. "The pixies won't leave much of Bluebottle for the coppers to find. I'm my own master once more."

"What of me? Planning on turning me over to them?" He glanced around him.

"The thought crossed my mind." Tupp took a long sip of the mulled wine, enjoying its warmth and spices. "But you did save my life, and for that I'm thankful and forgiving. Your debt is paid."

The boy looked disappointed. "So that's it? After what we just did... Bloody hell, after all I've seen of late—"

"Relax," Tupp motioned towards the boy's untouched cup. "Have a drink." The fey was pleased at Lind's complaint. He had wondered if the boy would simply disappear after the night's adventure and found himself surprised to have grown so fond of Lind.

"At least let me pay for my own." The boy reached into his shirt and withdrew several small bags that he dropped onto the table between them.

Tupp stared at the familiar bags a moment, utterly astounded. "Where did you get these?"

"Oh, a good cracksman never leaves without a little something. Found them in that back room." Lind reached for his cup and sniffed before drinking. He smacked his lips in appreciation. "Open them up. They're filled with gold dust."

Tupp laughed and undid the ties to one. His fingers dug inside to lift up a pinch of glittering powder. "My boy, this isn't gold." He leaned in close. "It's glamour and worth a great deal to the Folk."

Lind's eyes widened. "So, what are we going to do with it?"

"We?" Tupp chuckled good-naturedly.

"Aye." The boy hefted one of the bags. "We worked well together."

"And you'd want to be partners with one of the Folk?" Tupp wrapped both his hands around Lind's. "It's risky, I warn you." He looked into the boy's eyes, almost mesmerized by their merry green.

Lind answered with a grin. "What's life without a little danger? Partners it is."

AUTHOR'S NOTE

In my junior year at Tulane, I enrolled in the Victorian Short Story. I better remember the professor's wiry eyebrows, oiled mustache, and fondness for the term "homosocial," than anything by Hardy or Trollope. October's assignment was deconstructing a short piece by Sir Arthur Conan Doyle and most students began reading the Sherlock Holmes stories. With my fascination for the macabre, the obvious choice was "Lot No. 249."

This story of a deranged Oxford student who animates a blackened, gaunt mummy through ancient sorcery was a source of inspiration for the 1932 Universal film. And like all literature, the story suffers from nineteenth-century language easily misconstrued:

> "Bellingham, however, appeared to have taken a fancy to his rough-spoken neighbour, and made his advances in such a way that he could hardly be repulsed without absolute brutality. Twice he called to thank Smith for his assistance, and many times afterwards he looked in with books, papers, and such other civilities as two bachelor neighbours can offer each other"

I smirked at such prose. I envied Doyle. If I'd turned in a manuscript with similar "homosocial" descriptions, everyone in class would harbor suspicions (and right they would be).

THAT SAME OCTOBER, *Zeta Psi threw a Halloween party. Mike had joined the fraternity the previous fall and I was so jealous of the time he spent with them that I pledged the next semester. The brothers learned how I idolized Mike, but none of them suspected how deeply I ached for him.*

But Mike never stayed with anything once the challenge was gone. In his closet was diving gear that had not been worn since he'd been certified, there was always another girl for another night, and he deactivated from the fraternity less than a month after my own initiation. He had few constants at Tulane other than me being his friend and roommate and I think now codependence allowed me to last as long as I did with him.

The fraternity punished me for choosing to live off-campus with Mike and not at the house with them. They never told me when they scheduled the photographer. They never visited or called the apartment. And I was the only brother they refused to allow to mentor a pledge. It was as if they were forcing me to deactivate as well.

I only agreed to attend the party because some of the pledges asked me. Nothing flattering. A pledge needed the signatures of all the active brothers. Some brothers withheld their signatures until the pledge had performed a ridiculous task. I suppose something as Herculean as riding the streetcar fifteen minutes to my off-campus apartment and actually getting to know me was out of the question. No, I had to come to them.

NIGHTS WRITING PAGE *after page picking apart the bones of Doyle's mummy inspired my costume. I purchased every roll of gauze the campus store stocked. My concession to camp was a black bowtie and domino mask that I hoped made me look a bit fresh on the town after years in the sarcophagus.*

But before I could dress, I had to help Mike with his costume, chosen at the last moment. A Roman senator. I spray-painted gold leaves from the dying tree out front of the apartment while he ripped apart a spare bed sheet.

He was restless; his favorite bar, The Bons Temps Rouler, was offering dollar Pumpkin Pie shots at sundown, yet I coaxed from him stories of past Halloween adventures.

Soon after we first met, I learned how easy it was to distract Mike with questions. He loved to brag about past exploits, and I could sit there, admiring every inch of his body while he stripped down to change clothes without either of us ashamed. And so, I could touch the warm skin of his bared chest and shoulder more than necessary as I tested the knots on his makeshift toga.

It began as a dare. A friend's bothersome little brother had to cross through a graveyard, from front gate to rear, at midnight. If he did, there'd be beer—Boss Cox Double Dark, which poured the color of a chocolate-covered ruby once the foam cleared—as many bottles as he could drink. But Mike knew the thirteen year old wanted the real prize: status in the eyes of his brother's peers.

They didn't warn him they'd be dressed as ragged zombies and hiding behind the headstones. And no one anticipated rain.

Drops of rain spattered the beer bottles Mike had emptied while waiting for the boy to pass by him. He stuck them neck first into the wet earth by the gravestone. Most of the greasy makeup he'd worn had been wiped away.

He heard the boy's screams and readied himself. When the boy ran past, Mike sprang. The mud caught the boy's sneakers and Mike gripped his legs. They struggled and then the boy kicked Mike in the mouth. The pain went through his skull and sent a spike through whatever judgment the Double Dark had left. Mike twisted the boy's foot and didn't stop until the boy screamed and the bone snapped.

The others came running. They found Mike carrying the boy. Mike wouldn't talk to anyone until he'd reached the rear gate, where the boy's brother had fallen asleep in his pickup truck.

Every night for six weeks, until the cast came off, Mike would drive to the brothers' house and throw rocks at the boy's window until he slipped out and drank the bottle of beer Mike brought him.

Mike admired his costume in the full-length mirror attached to his door.

I wondered if the boy he'd hurt ever came to dread the sound of pebbles striking the window pane. Did he worry what Mike might do to him if he hesitated climbing down the trellis while burdened with a cast? I imagined them sitting together, the grass beneath them cold and stiff with frost, as Mike twisted the cap of yet another beer. He would shove it into boy's hands.

He'd done so with me. Maybe laugh if the boy couldn't finish the bottle. Maybe lift the very end and force him to swallow or choke on the beer. He'd done so with me.

When he left the apartment, I sat on his bed. I stripped off my clothes and then slipped under his covers. Mike changed the bed sheets once a semester and the thought of him lying in them night after night calmed me when I became anxious. When he went away for the weekend, I'd spend most of it sleeping in his bed. I did not want to attend a party where I'd not feel welcome. But Halloween deserved celebrating. I hoped some trace of his glamour would seep from the bedding through my skin and settle in my bones.

I took a shower, then dressed in an undershirt, briefs and socks. All white in case the wrappings tore. The gauze would not stay tight against my limbs. I found a bag of petrified flour in the kitchen cabinet and chiseled it apart in the bathtub with the help of the hot water tap. And when the bandages ran out, I used toilet paper and mâchéd myself armor that resembled a mummy.

NEARLY ALL OF Tulane's Greek houses were on Broadway Street, nearly an hour walk from the apartment. Parts of me had unraveled. The cacophony of multiple Halloween parties echoed down the block.

I never knew how the Zeta Psi house remained standing. The porch was half-rotten, the doors askew, every floorboard buckled and groaned, and cracks patterned every wall.

In the foyer, a diver in a wetsuit waved a beer-pong tube at me. His eyes looked wild as he shoved the snorkeling mask up to his forehead. One of the pledges. I couldn't remember his name. Perhaps Chuck or Scott. Acne scarred his cheeks, his nose had once been broken, but those blue eyes—a Caribbean-atoll shade of blue—made amends for his tatty features.

With the makeshift plaster on my face I couldn't smile without cracking, so I nodded and made my way to the littered bar. I pushed aside empty bottles, hoping for a clean plastic cup.

Look who showed.

My fraternity brothers drank spiked punch that left their lips slashed red.

Mike with you?

Where's your better half?

For all their sarcasm, I knew that if Mike stepped through the front door, they would be slapping his back, plying him with drinks, and soon begging for him to be part of their motley gang once more. Mike's glamour was ever so hard to resist; after a few minutes in his company, you ached to please him, to touch him, to be his disciple. Perhaps they were all jealous of me.

A pledge wearing ragged clothing—maybe he was a Dickensian orphan—slapped his palm on the bar. You owe me a signature.

I doubt you could read hieroglyphics, I told him.

Something grasped my neck and pulled me a step back. Diver Pledge had hooked me with his snorkel.

He whispered in my ear, You're my first kidnap victim. Or the stiff gauze wrapped around my head made it seem like a whisper. I worried that the bandages would not hide my growing hard-on.

Kidnapping was the one acceptable act of rebelliousness allowed pledges. If they could, as a group, abduct a brother—who could never refuse them— they'd be rewarded. Of course, they had to treat the brother well, and most kidnap victims ended up drunk.

Six pledges led me out of the house. They brought with them bottles of bum wine, drainpipe liquor. The Diver had not released me and walked backwards, which seemed so quirky and confident that I found myself all the more entranced with him.

We reached Audubon Park, next to campus, a wide swathe of greenery and curved macadam paths all but lost in the darkness. New Orleans still clutched its humidity, its heat, well into October. The pledges twisted off caps and threw them into the grass. They passed the Black Currant and Orange Jubilee around. As I drank the sickly-sweet wine, I hoped my liver was safely stored in a canopic jar somewhere.

They had me laughing, lost and distracted from why they'd needed me, until one, the pauper, took out his pledge manual. And, after I scribbled a signature on their backs, my mood soured like the cheap wine in my stomach. I was soon abandoned.

Except by the Diver. He remained behind, leaning against a massive oak. No signature?

He shrugged. Not sure if I have my book. His mask muffled his voice. Drunk and unsure what to do with the bottle he held, the Diver fumbled to reach the zipper of his wetsuit. Thought I had it under here...

A pledge found without book or badge would be hazed unmercifully.

I turned him around. He stumbled a bit before pressing his empty hand against the rough bark of the tree.

In one smooth motion, I unzipped him down to his waist. The neoprene opened to reveal a strip of slick skin that had been marinating for hours and hours in sweat. I peeled back one side. A scattering of inflamed pimples made an angry constellation over his shoulders and back.

I don't see it. I suspected he didn't have on underwear.

He didn't respond.

Dare I blame being drunk myself? Or was I foolhardy because Halloween, my favorite night of the year, offered me a trick, a treat? I slipped a hand underneath the curling neoprene suit. My fingers sluiced through sweat as they slipped around to his chest. Then, after feeling how he sucked in a breath, I slid my hand lower, down to his stomach. Rough hairs tickled my fingertips.

He groaned and tugged off his mask. But to keep balanced, his other arm went back. The bottle he held struck me hard in the mouth.

Pain kissed me deeply, even after I stumbled and fell to the ground. My fingers went to the spaces where I once had teeth. The gauze bandages soaked up blood.

His apologies came quick and eager as he helped me stand. I'd never spit before and found myself forced to again and again, as we stumbled through campus, or I'd cough on the blood pooling in my mouth. We passed other students who must have thought the red spilling down my chin onto my chest fake. At the student health center, I let Diver go.

MIKE TEASED ME about the missing incisors. I sought comfort in Percocet and a dental appointment for a lower bridge. For the next few nights, I'd lie in bed and drift off, hoping to be awoken by the sound of rocks thrown at my bedroom window. But the Diver never came for me, and I couldn't bring myself to step foot in the fraternity house again.

TEARJERKER

Thisday

GAIL HATES BEING outside when it rains vinegar. She doubts the hags' assurances that it clears the skin and removes warts; as a child, she put chicken bones in vinegar to discover days later they would be all rubbery. She wipes the wet hair from her face, grimacing at the sour trickle that slips past her lips. Her hands move to the pocket of her jeans, checking again for the plastic bottle of aspirin from the shelter.

She stumbles down the block, her sneakers sodden and her feet cold as she steps in puddles. The weak light coming from the sky with its brown clouds makes the street look unfamiliar, and for a moment, before hearing the recorded saxophone, she thinks she might be lost.

Then she spots the faded awning up ahead and the white stonework. The doors to the dilapidated hotel are left open until nightfall.

Bulbs sputter in the old crystal chandeliers in the lobby. A quiet line of people stands waiting to reach the front desk. Each holds something they think has value. Layers of wet clothing drip and saturate the frayed Persian rug. From hidden speakers comes more wailing brass.

She feels feverish inside the stifling-warm lobby. Gail's soaked sweater hangs about her like a lead vest. Through the line of people, she catches sight of Brennan. The little girl sits atop the front desk, her small legs hanging over the side. The hags have dressed her in the lemony-yellow sundress with lace trim, her blonde hair held back with a white scrunchie. One of the Grace sisters stands beside her, and, as Gail watches, the old woman grins and pinches Brennan's cheeks with both hands. Not fondly, but hard enough to turn the little girl's face red and the hag's knuckles bone-white. Brennan begins crying, and the Grace sister strokes her chin. "There, there, well done, dear," she coos, before lifting a porcelain teacup to catch the tears. "That will do nicely."

The hags wear brightly colored flannel nightgowns with slippers. Their weak, watery eyes resemble a hound dog's.

Next to the first Grace is her twin, holding aloft a vintage hypodermic, the sort that Gail has seen in black-and-white movies, all glass and shiny chrome. The hag's lips form a small "o" as she focuses on refilling the needle from the teacup.

Gail tries not to stare as the needle slips into the next in line. The smell of those waiting makes her want to retch. Being a tearfreak is no excuse for poor hygiene. Once she is back working for the hags, she'll draw the addicts' baths. She can scrounge for salts and scented soaps. Everyone will appreciate her.

She climbs up the grand staircase, trying not to catch her feet on the ripped runner. A middle-aged man in denim overalls plods up the steps. One hand trails along the wallpaper; he has not rolled down his sleeve after receiving the injection.

The tearfreaks don't always reach their rooms, and some collapse on the landing or a hallway. The hags hate when that happens and have told Gail how slovenly it leaves the hotel. They order her to put the addicts to bed.

Gail will come back later to see if the man needs help; she wants one last conversation with Alexander. He needs the aspirin.

—

Days Past

ALL THE ROOMS on the hotel's third floor (the stairs skipped the second floor, and no matter how many times she tried, Gail couldn't find her way there) were numbered 83. The hags forbade her from venturing onto the fourth or fifth floors. The elevators didn't work, hadn't since reality fell away last year, and the only way to reach the upper levels was by gloomy passages along the servant's stairwell. Ever since she began working for the hags months ago, Gail had thought of herself as a servant girl and explored the hotel whenever possible.

That was how she came upon Alexander on the fourth floor in room 450. Or maybe the fifth floor, room 540. Sometimes the numbers changed when she wasn't looking.

She had been scooping out deviled ham from a jar with her fingers and roaming the dim hallway of doors when she overhead a Grace sister speaking.

"There once was an old woman who lived in a vinegar bottle? Not a very believable beginning to my story."

Gail peered around the door. The hag sat on one of the uncomfortable wooden chairs found in many of the rooms. She leaned over a young man lying on top of the sheets, one of her gnarled hands lifting up the front of his bathrobe. Underneath, he was naked, though someone had written in red ink all over his skin. Even the soles of his feet had words: *I shall be so happy living here* up the right foot and down the left.

"I think you could at least come up with a better ending for me," said the hag. "Ungrateful."

The young man grunted. Maybe groaned.

When the hag stood, Gail slipped away into the next room's welcome darkness. She licked her fingers clean, then slipped the empty jar into her pocket. She heard the creak of the floorboards as the Grace sister passed by. They always creaked, and Gail wondered if their footfalls aged the hotel step by step.

She counted to a hundred before entering the young man's room. Under the white terrycloth robe, his chest rose and fell. The writing had vanished from his skin, which looked pale and drawn to the bone. He might have been handsome if someone hadn't shaved off all his hair—not just scalped him but plucked clean his eyebrows and lashes as well.

He opened his eyes. *Who is there?* bled onto his forehead.

His marred body marked him as Afflicted, one of the caste changed for the worse by the Fall. She had never been so close to one before. "Doesn't that hurt?"

He nodded. She felt better knowing it pained him. That made sense. Too many things about the hotel, about the Fallen Area, never did.

"I wonder why the sisters never mentioned you." She sat down beside him on the bed.

I am their keepsake. Alexander.

"I'm Gail. I do all the dull stuff for the hags. It looks like they are doing a very poor job of keeping you." She doubted he weighed more than a hundred pounds.

Truly, scrolled across his chin and neck.

"I don't mind reading you, but it's hard to have a long conversation. I'd have to peek and we only just met." She nearly giggled.

Alexander opened his mouth. He had very white teeth but no tongue. She could not see any scar tissue.

"Sorry."

Could you bring me something to eat?

"Sure." She regretted finishing off the deviled ham. Real food could be hard to come by Inside. She had taken the jar late last night from behind the front desk; one of the tearfreaks must have brought it as payment for a fix. The tangy paste would have been easy for Alexander to swallow without a tongue. She wondered if he could still chew.

The power didn't work in the hotel's vast kitchen, but the hags had bartered with an anthvoke to fix the refrigerator, a massive bone-white relic that lurked in the corner of the kitchen like a dusty fossil. While it worked without electricity, shaking and humming, they must have cheated the Talented out of his payment, for the refrigerator conjured only chilled condiments. The hags did not seem to mind, and their breath was always a miasma of sweet and sour.

Gail never trusted any of the Talented. They cheated at surviving with their unfair gifts. Awakening dead household appliances might seem pathetic, but it gave anthvokes an edge over the normals like her, who had to contend with life in the Fallen Area. She regretted not leaving Philly before the immense concrete walls had been erected, quarantining what the rest of the country considered a "reality infection." The early days of the Fall had seemed exciting, but the novelty had been worn away by constant uncertainty—streets could misdirect from one day to the next, what had once been a safe spot to crash might become risky to walk past. The Talented frightened her, too. The Afflicteds' bodies no longer worked as they once did, but the Talented could work the chaos Inside as they pleased, like selfish magic.

The rules of life changed constantly. She could only persevere. The hags paid little, but the hotel's quirks didn't threaten. She helped herself whenever possible.

Gail tugged hard on the refrigerator's cool metal handle. Jars and bottles crammed the shelves. She started rooting through them. Colman's Mustard. Alaga Pickle Syrup. Mack's Cider Vinegar. Anything an anthvoke awoke had to be vintage. She found Bengal Club Chutney and a can of chocolate sauce.

"Snick-snacking so early, dear?" One of the sisters stood in the doorway.

Gail shrugged. She had never mastered the quick lie.

"We need you to clean the last 83. Poor Mr. Theo's constitution isn't what it used to be. We may have to water the tears down next time."

Gail nodded, hiding her annoyance. Mr. Theo should be the last one taking tears. The old man couldn't move without a litany of groans. "I'll take care of it."

When she stripped the bed of the soiled sheets, a tiny gilded case slipped to the floor. She picked it up, listening to its rattle and fingering the scratched enameled terrier on the top. Her thumb flicked the latch and she counted seven tiny pills. What do old men have? Hardened arteries? High blood pressure? Gail promised under her breath to give the case back to Mr. Theo when she saw him later in the week.

She felt guilty it took so long to return to Alexander and apologized several times. He needed help eating. Gail had to tip the chutney, allowing small chunks and liquid into his mouth, then water brought from the sink in the deviled ham jar. Like a ventriloquist dummy, he could "talk" while swallowing.

I was the sister's first attraction. My stories filled the lobby.

"Before they found Brennan?" Gail wiped his lips and chin clean.

Yes. The little woebegone.

"I once sneaked a sip from her tea cup. It tasted so sweet, made me choke. I fell asleep and dreamed." Gail remembered the sensation on her tongue, how it made her shiver all over.

What of?

"Snowglass Night. Sitting in front of my television set, eager for news on what happened to the neighborhood. Some cable network. The announcer spoke to me. Not like normal, he actually answered my questions. Told me how bad the rain would be the next day and I should wear galoshes. Do they still make yellow rubber boots? Anyways, the announcer had an overbite and a bad toupee, and he had finished telling me that people were disappearing in Philly, and then static interrupted him. The screen had the black and white confetti snow, like all the plugs had been pulled but the power. I went to my window and knew that sets for blocks around were snowed in and always would be."

Sometimes I think I overhear the dreams of the addicts. Alexander grimaced as the words rose. *I remember how contented they were listening to my stories read aloud. So quiet, so still, with smiles.*

Gail normally slept well, especially if she visited Brennan before bed. But finding Alexander provoked her thoughts, leaving her restless on the mattress in the grand ballroom. She turned over, and one foot slipped out from beneath the blanket. The marble tile sent a chill through her.

Why would the hags keep Alexander? They had always seemed disgusted with Afflicteds, turning away any that entered the lobby. Gail never minded them, not the ones with minor deformities, such as the girl with glass hair Gail once glimpsed waiting outside the stalls of the Food Auction.

She closed her eyes and tried to drift off while envisioning crimson writing covering the insides of her own eyelids. She thought of him stranded in that bed. Were they punishing him? The thought made her anxious about what might one day happen to her.

＝

THE SISTERS HAD instructed that Gail hand wash all of Brennan's clothes. They made her add rainwater to each rinse, so the colors wouldn't fade. On dry weeks, she took vinegar from the refrigerator.

When not shedding a tear, Brennan was kept in her room. Brennan sat on the floor in pink pajamas and fuzzy slippers, not far from where the metal secured her leash. She looked up when Gail brought the clean laundry. "Hello."

"Hey, kid." She began putting away the clothes in the closet.

"You've seen the Bookman." Brennan's tone blended whine and accusation perfectly.

Gail stopped. "You know about him?"

Brennan nodded. "Yep. He's ugly."

"Aren't you the sweetheart?" Not for the first time did Gail wonder what the girl really was. Not truly Afflicted, as she seemed normal except for her tears.

"Why don't you like me?" Tiny lips pouted.

Gail sighed. "But I do." Practiced lies came naturally to her. She left the laundry and took Brennan into her arms. "Now do I get my taste?" Her mouth grew wet with anticipation.

Brennan shook her head, tickling Gail's face with blonde hair.

Gail did not raise her voice. That hadn't worked in the past. Brennan might hide under the bed, and then Gail would have to drag her out by the tether. "Mean little girls grow up ugly."

"Like the sisters?"

"Like the sisters." Gail hugged Brennan. "So?"

Brennan bit down on her lower lip. She had an overbite. Tears formed at the corners of her eyes. When they traveled down her puffy cheek, Gail eagerly licked them away.

The cloying taste made her tongue feel lacquered, and she fought a coughing spell. She let go of Brennan and grabbed the laundry basket. By the time she reached the hallway, she could feel her insides glowing. She took a few more steps, and then dawdled under a sputtering wall sconce. Her skin tingled, and she stared at her arms, wondering if words lurked just under the surface, the serifs scratching to be set free.

=

Visits with Alexander became as necessary as treats from Brennan. Gail listened as he told marvelous things, secrets taken from the Grace sisters. They had been beautiful once, with dancers' legs, swinging their hips in simpático with jazz from the hotel speakers. She read that pariah dogs patrolled the Fallen Area, meeting in a cabal of mutts. That one of the tearfreaks spied for the outside world, but his reports rambled with lachrymose dreams. Alexander seemed eager for attention even when it pained him to write. When she left, he could stir a little and lifted an arm to take the water glass.

She decided to spend the following night with Alexander until her eyes became blurry. Perhaps he would offer her a lullaby. She held tight to the banister as she climbed to the fourth floor. Creaking sounds came from up ahead. Half-illuminated by the light of Alexander's room, the hags drifted down the hall in pale, quilted housecoats.

Gail hoped they would walk past his room on their way to bed. She never knew where they slept. But they stopped outside of 450. Each sister reached for the other's satin belt, loosening it. Their coats fell with a velvety sigh to the worn carpet. Bare breasts sagged, but the skin on their thighs looked taut, the buttocks firm. They held hands and walked inside.

Gail ran back to the ballroom. She lay on her back and stared at the ceiling all night and shuddered whenever she thought she heard a sound. She told herself that forgetting Alexander would be best.

She busied herself with her chores and visits to Brennan. When Mr. Theo came to the lobby empty-handed, begging for tears, she watched the hags level a revolver at his chest and threaten to ruin the rugs unless he left the hotel. She never offered to return his little case, still in her pocket.

When that afternoon's line of tearfreaks dwindled away, Gail swept the floor. With the broom she maneuvered the trail of dirt into arcs, reminiscent of Alexander's handwriting. By the time she had finished with the lobby, she had to sit down on the bottom step and catch her breath. Her hands trembled, and when she rubbed them, they felt bony and worn.

Brennan ran up to her. She lacked her leash. "They want to see you." Brennan looked back over her shoulder in the direction of the hotel bar.

"Trouble double." She curtsied once and then giggled while running up the staircase.

The mahogany-paneled walls of the bar might have once suggested a warm opulence, but now the room seemed restrictive and stuffy. Normally it was kept padlocked, as the hags did not want anyone to steal what little liquor remained. Gail had discovered the combination soon after she started working. She discovered she enjoyed single malts around then as well.

Sitting together on a burgundy leather chaise, the sisters cupped crystal tumblers of scotch in their laps.

"We heard you were a thief." The left Grace slurred her words.

Gail had never seen either drunk before; the sight of their wet lips bothered her more than the accusation.

The twin dipped a finger into her glass and swirled the drink around the rim, creating a brief chime. "You think being young and pretty masks cleverness."

What did they know? She tried to recall everything she had taken.

"You've been feeding our Book."

"He has a name."

Both made an odd sound of derision, almost a wheeze.

"I'm not the one keeping a man prisoner."

Another chuff. "Who's locked and who's the locket?" The left Grace stabbed towards Gail and spilt her drink. "His stories have left us old."

"Sister, you're still beautiful." The right Grace stroked the other's face.

"I'm taking him away." But her words sounded hollow to her own ears. She had no idea where she could take him. Yet the thought of sharing Alexander with the hags—and the memory of seeing them disrobe and saunter into his room—pained her.

"Did he fuck you?"

The right Grace smirked while threading her fingers through her sister's gray hair. "His dick is shaped like a fountain pen."

"Horrible nib."

"Hurts like hell."

As Gail ran from the bar to the lobby, she heard one of them call out, "We're the only ones that never tire of his stories. We kept him. Kept him safe."

=

WHEN THE WIND struck her bare arms, Gail regretted being so quick to leave the warmth of the hotel. She wandered aimlessly down the next two blocks, telling herself that in the morning the hags would be sober and reasonable. They'd take her back if she promised to avoid Alexander.

She could see her breath rising in front of her. The closest doorway led into a liquor store. Shards of glass covered much of the floor. The shelves had been ransacked, probably ages ago. Down one aisle, she found and shook clean a banner for Pennsylvania wineries. Wrapped up in it, she lay on some old wooden pallets and tried to sleep.

She stirred well after morning. Whatever soured wine remaining at the bottom of some broken bottles seemed to have coated the inside of her throat. Her head ached with something akin to a hangover.

The hags wore cheerful floral nighties in the morning. They scowled when she walked into the lobby.

"We thought of you like a daughter."

"Now you're far too wayward for our liking," said the other and motioned with the revolver at the door. The gunmetal gleamed as if oiled.

"My stuff—" Gail had one foot on the staircase when she heard the safety's click. The sisters tsk-ed, and Brennan muffled giggles behind a small hand. The unkempt line of addicts broke apart when they noticed Gail crying, and she had to struggle through hands grasping to reach her face.

She wandered the neighborhood. A place that sold tea looked inviting until she remembered they had thrown her out after catching her stealing from a woman's open purse. She napped briefly in a deep doorway until nudged.

The couple standing over her had kind faces, which worried her while she blinked away sleep, but they insisted she would be safer at the shelter. She wondered how she could not have known such a place existed, but then she had never dared explore every twisted street Inside.

The shelter had once been a posh Cuban restaurant she could have never afforded before the Fall. The walls remained a warm orange stucco decorated with framed vintage prints of buxom women leaning or stretching with cigars nearby. But now they looked down upon dingy cots and blankets and tables cluttered with pots and trays. Ashtrays of polished, cloudy marble were stacked in spots and held the remains of candles.

There, the nurse, a pudgy short woman with close-cropped hair, offered Gail warm clothes from a donation box and a couch to rest on. The wool sweater smelled musty and hung like a tent on her frame. The others staying at the shelter eyed her warily. She drank salty soup and considered asking if the workers were volunteers or were they paid.

When the nurse was distracted helping a scrawny goth boy delivering packages, Gail snooped around, finding the infirmary behind a hastily hung curtain. She picked up a lighter that weighed down some letters. Her thumb traced over the engraving—*Aroma*—then flicked the wheel and created a tiny flame. It had to be worth something. She palmed it before the nurse could come back.

"I think I need some air," she told the woman.

Gail carried on a long conversation with the hags as she retraced her steps to the hotel. They told her how sorry they felt over casting her out and offered treats. Brennan would be so relieved to have her back; the sweet tears would flow down that round face. Tears just for her.

When Gail walked through the doors, the hags waved at her, beckoning towards the front desk. She held up her offering, sparking the lighter's flame. "Here, a present."

"Aww, dear, we thought you might come back for a dose." One of the hags rubbed Gail's arm warmly, while the other filled the needle from the cup.

"You look so haggard. Have you not been sleeping well?"

Gail slid up the sweater's sleeve as the sister came closer with the needle. But the point dipped before it broke skin and the tears squirted out to land on the floor.

Gail yelped, as if she had been jabbed to the bone, and fell to her knees. She barely stopped herself from clutching the damp rug.

"Maybe you need to curl up with a good book, dear."

She wrapped her arms around her torso as proof against their cackles, but still they stung. With nowhere else to go, she returned to the shelter. She needed a bit of care before figuring out what she might do. Normals who had no role in the Fallen Area ended up lost and hungry. Roaming Inside was dangerous. More than people had been altered. She had overheard too many rumors of carnivorous alleys and debris.

That evening, she woke soaked in sweat. Her fingers twitched, her body burned as if the acid in her stomach had spilled. Gail could not recall where she was, and panic filled her for several minutes until her eyes adjusted to the darkness and she remembered. She shouted out for the nurse. Groans and curses of disturbed sleepers echoed. The syrupy medicine the nurse brought slowly soothed her.

Stabbing pain heralded each motion the next day. Even breathing took effort. She found a hand mirror and stared long at her reflection. Had the skin around her eyes always looked crinkled? The other women staying at the shelter laughed at what they must think was vanity, but Gail knew what had happened. The hags had warned her about Alexander too late. She felt ancient.

The nurse hassled her with questions about drugs. Gail screamed to be left alone. She knew the sisters would never let her see Brennan again. She wanted nothing more than to hold the girl close, to nuzzle and kiss that soft face. Then everything would be right again.

The rain fell, and her pain worsened. Arthritis, she was sure. Her trembling fingers went to the faux-gold case in her pocket. Bent low to hide the contents from the others, she considered taking one of Mr. Theo's mystery pills. If she stared hard, letters gradually appeared on their surface, as if she had palmed tiny bits of Alexander's weird flesh.

"What is Lanoxin?" Gail asked the nurse, when the woman came to check on her. She kept her treasure hidden underneath the blanket.

Suspicion narrowed the nurse's eyes. "Digitalis. Foxglove. You're too young to worry about such things."

"I thought I heard one of the others asking for it."

"I hope not. It's for people with weak hearts." The nurse leaned forward and whispered, "How's the withdrawal?"

Gail shook her head. The woman didn't understand. Gail didn't crave Alexander's words anymore. She needed to stop reading him. The hags, too. Maybe without their Book they'd all become young again. He must have a terrible heart to hurt them all so. Maybe she wouldn't have to feed him all the little pills. "Do you have an aspirin?" she asked.

=

Thisday

The hags never see her climb the staircase. Or maybe they approve of her plan. Yes, Gail is sure they must. Maybe Brennan, too.

Gail raps her sore hands on Alexander's open door. He stares at her from the bed. She offers her best smile.

"Let's talk." She jiggles the bottle. The Lanoxin rattles along with the aspirin.

The sisters told me you left.

"It hurts, I know." She grits her teeth while prying off the cap. It takes three attempts, and she struggles not to gasp by the end. "Here." She brings the pills to his lips. He opens his mouth, and she makes sure to place them on his molars. He grinds his teeth.

"Now tell me a story." She sits down on the chair. As the letters flourish over his skin, she tries not to shiver in anticipation of reading his ending.

AUTHOR'S NOTE

My FIRST SEXUAL experience had been so disastrous that it left me depressed for months. Mike demanded to know the reason for my being so morose, and so I came out to him. I didn't dare tell my true feelings for him, though.

He began to sob. I'd always thought his reaction would be screams—and anticipated he might hit me—but the sight of him breaking down was awful. I felt as if I'd betrayed our friendship. He left the apartment and didn't return until the next morning. Afterwards, he barely spoke to me and was often away from the apartment.

I went to his graduation ceremony. And though he promised to do so, he did not attend mine.

So, when his mother told me that Mike had died on my twenty-first birthday, I didn't cry. I felt as if, by being the survivor, I'd won some twisted game we'd been forced to play. I may have even laughed after hanging up the phone.

But I could not stop talking about him to strangers.

WELL WISHING

THE SALESMAN TASTED the dust in the air streaming through the open windows as he drove down the dirt road. The Ford Fairlane's faulty air-conditioning, wheezing, failed to chill the interior against a blinding August sun. The right front tire popped suddenly. The car shuddered, especially the steering wheel. The salesman cursed as he guided the sedan to the side of the road.

Outside, he bent down on ailing knees to look at the flat tire. His bright red tie hung like a panting dog's tongue in the heat of the late day. He cursed more on his way to the trunk. There had to be a spare somewhere underneath the sample boxes. But he couldn't find one.

He remembered passing a farmhouse. They'd have a phone, though he'd rather have a faucet to splash cold water over his head. He took his briefcase and suit jacket, out of habit. He didn't bother locking the car; if someone wanted to come along and take the plumbing-supply brochures and sales charts, they were welcome to do so. Few clients had this season. He rolled up the sleeves of his damp dress shirt and began walking.

There once was a lonely farmer's son who visited the heads of his lovers in an old wishing well.

The salesman knocked on the farmhouse door. The wooden boards of the porch creaked underneath his feet. A gruff and grim face peered out when the door opened slightly.

"You look like a feller that sells somethin'." The man looked ready to spit from tobacco-stained lips.

"No, wait." The salesman reached out and the palm of his hand smacked against the closing door. "My car broke down a mile from here. I just want to use your phone."

A softer, gentler voice spoke from somewhere behind the man. "Pa, let the poor man in." Thick fingers with brightly painted nails reached around and pulled the door aside.

The salesman offered his Closing Grin, the most sincere expression in his limited repertoire. The frowning old man remained blocking the threshold. A young girl beside him, shorter and stouter but very pretty with long blond hair, took hold of one of the farmer's overall straps and pulled him back.

"Forgive Pa. He likes them canvassers 'bout as much as he does Eisenhower." She reached out and took the salesman's arm. Her strong grip guided him into a parlor. Dust motes danced in the shreds of sunlight from open windows.

"I'll bring you a glass of iced lemonade." She pushed him down onto the tufted sofa. His rump felt an inch or so of padding before reaching the hard wood backing. He immediately missed the sedan's front seat, which felt like an opulent throne in comparison.

The old man leaned into the parlor's doorway. "Kids are trustin'. Too trustin' for my likin'. What's wrong with the car?"

"Flat tire."

"George can tow ya into town. Has a plum garage."

The girl returned with a sweating glass. She leaned down farther than necessary, offering a view of her bosom. The salesman made sure to reach for the glass with his left hand, mindful to show off the gold wedding ring. The girl took notice and her lips puckered. After the salesman took a sip his lips puckered as well. He managed to force a slight smile. "The phone?" Swallowing, half his voice seemed lost.

"In the kitchen," said the farmer.

"Stay for dinner," said the daughter.

They led the salesman to where a black Bakelite beast hung on the wall. It looked like the misbegotten child of the iron stove across the room.

Whenever he could, the farmer's son would sneak out of the house or away from his chores and go to the well. He had found it years ago, overgrown and empty, the faded Wishing Well sign on the ground. Three heads bobbed in the dark water now. He knew them well. The first belonged to the neighbor's boy. It was the favorite of the farmer's son, who would often comb the wet curly hair away from blue eyes. The second had been an accident. He shouldn't have been drinking with his sister Claire's beau that night. The third and most recent head had such heavy jowls often only the thick lips and dimpled chin would surface and gulp air. The local Justice of the Peace, now just pieces.

The mechanic annoyed the salesman, but conveyed the sense that yes, he would tow the car and yes, he would change the tire, and for an extra fee and some extra time, could fix the air-conditioning.

That meant the salesman would have to find someplace to spend the night. He opened his wallet to the farmer. He had no idea if the farmer even knew who Andrew Jackson was. "I could sleep on your sofa if you don't have a spare bed." Though he instantly regretted the idea. The floorboards or the dirt outside might be softer. Out of the corner of his eye, the salesman caught a glimpse of the daughter twirling a lock of hair around her fingers.

The back screen door opened and a short young man walked into the kitchen. The rivulets of sweat that ran down his forehead and neck streaked dirty skin. A few tufts of dried grass clung to close-cropped hair. Like the old farmer, he wore overalls, but nothing else.

He snatched the glass of lemonade the salesman had set down. He drained it in one long drink. Drops of condensation fell onto the top of his chest, mixing with the sweat to reveal tanned skin under caked dust.

The salesman found himself staring. Habit made him twist the warm gold ring around and around on his finger.

"My boy," said the farmer with a grunt.

"Dan." The young man had curving wet lips. "You sellin' somethin'?"

"No." The salesman found his mouth dry. He regretted not getting more of the sour lemonade. "Just had a bit of car trouble."

"Trouble happens a lot around here." Dan wiped his forehead clear with the glass.

His sister punched him in the arm. "No need to be rude."

The farmer snatched the twenty-dollar bill from the salesman's hand. "We got an extra room. Belonged to Gran before she passed. You can sleep there."

Without another word, Dan returned to the outdoors, which made sense to the salesman; the young man looked like a wild thing. The girl began to putter about the kitchen, taking down pots and pans, reaching into the humming refrigerator. She gave the salesman a wink when she bent over to add wood to the stove.

The salesman followed after the farmer, up creaking stairs and down a dark hallway to the last room. It looked like no one had been inside in decades. The salesman sneezed twice at the smell of must and age. A faded quilt covered the bed.

"Even though I took your money, know I'll be listenin'. Beds squeak in this house," said the farmer.

"Sorry?"

"I mean to have my daughter Claire married to the right man, not some slick. You even think of payin' her a midnight visit and I'll introduce you to the other members of the house. Holland and Holland."

The salesman laid a hand on the bed. The rise of disturbed dust was accompanied by a cry of protest from the springs. "That would be a gun, I take it?"

The farmer nodded. "My beloved. Spits better than me." But the man still hawked his throat clear to land a brownish gob near the salesman's loafers.

The farmer's son knew that the heads in the well were his only friends. He would slip through the thick brush that surrounded the well and sit next to the cool stone walls, one hand draped over the side so his fingers could splash the water. He would call out to the heads and they would rise to the surface. The first, his first love too, came quickest, rising like a pink champagne bubble. Then his sister's boyfriend, and finally, after many taps on the surface, Justice. As he talked, they would smack their lips, reminding him of hungry pet goldfish he had won as a child one county fair. Those had died real quick, but not the heads. Sometimes, if the son leaned in far enough and brought his ear close to them, he could hear them weakly speak his name and ask for favors. Mostly the heads wanted company.

After thirty years selling plumbing supplies throughout the Midwest, the salesman knew his way around bathrooms. The same bad jokes at the annual sales conference in Chicago: beefsteaks, cigars, and the stalls at Union Station men's room.

He recognized the clawfoot at the farmhouse as a Lang Slipper, model A. In 1941, the tub would have gleamed with fresh, white porcelain over wood; now it looked as dingy as he felt. He turned the faucets. The water spilling out stayed murky while he counted past ten, but remained hot. He tempered it with a splash from the cold water tap.

He stripped off his clothes, leaving his ring and watch on top of the commode. He sat in the tub as it filled, balancing soap on his wide, hairy stomach. The water that rose around the bar became cloudy and the smell of lemongrass reached his nose.

The salesman slipped further down into the tub and dunked his head underneath the water. Only for a few seconds that left the world warm and silent but for the slight whoosh of his hands moving through the bath. But when he came up and blinked away the sudsy water, the salesman saw the farmer's son sitting on the edge of the tub. One overall strap hung undone, exposing a portion of bare chest. The salesman would have been startled but for Dan's smile.

The young man looked freshly scrubbed, skin almost as golden as his hair from the sun. "Where have you been?"

The salesman didn't know exactly what answer the young man sought. He shrugged. "Both coasts and lots of nowhere in between."

"I've never left the farm."

The salesman let his wet hand rise to the tub edge not far from Dan's leg. One finger had a tan line.

"Always alone?" Dan held up the wedding band between his thumb and forefinger. The ring looked flimsy.

The salesman nodded. "A trick. The world caters to married men." He slid his hand along the porcelain glaze onto Dan's thigh. "But I'm not the marrying kind."

Dan nodded. "I know some tricks." He opened his mouth wide while leaning his head back. Then he dropped the gold ring in.

"Suppose that was a family heirloom." The salesman smirked, remembering how he had found the ring many years ago in a demo sink's P-trap. His first sales call. The client had laughed and wondered if Link & Grant Plumbing Supplies offered prizes, like the treat inside a Cracker Jack box, with every purchase.

"You can try and get it back." Dan half-leaned in, half-slid down, his mouth open to show the ring that glittered like a lure on the back of his tongue. The salesman reached out with dripping arms and pulled the Dan into the tub. Their faces pressed hard, mouths forceful. The salesman's tongue sought the ring almost as an afterthought of exploring new territory.

"Haven't found it yet," laughed Dan. He splashed more water about while squatting over the salesman and unbuckling the remaining denim strap. His torso had been kissed by sun and youth and now water, which made the skin gleam like bronze fixtures.

"Shhh." The sound slid out of the salesman like steam. "Your father—"

"Is in bed with the Hollands after visitin' Jim Beam a while in the kitchen. He wants you to stay away from my sister. I do too."

"I promise," said the salesman, who pressed his mouth back to the young man's chest. He heard Dan moan slightly and mutter, "It's best for all of us."

The farmer's son leaned over the well's edge to dip his fingertips in the cool water. Now and then one of the heads would idly bump against his hand. He noticed that the water's surface dimpled, before realizing tears fell from his face. He wiped his cheeks. The heads in the well were not enough. They could barely whisper. If lifted from the well, they'd become listless. The farmer's son wanted to hear a man, whether his own name grunted or gently said. He missed the feel of hands upon his body and of touching warm skin, tracing fingers through sweat. But the farmer's son could not escape. Not from the farm, with its daylight of endless chores and nighttime of quiet need. Not from the well, for fear that the heads would sink to the bottom and rest there like stones cast away. The land had belonged to the family for generations and owned him. His loneliness kept him at the well as much as it had brought the heads to the water.

The next day, the salesman sat on the rickety porch. Yesterday's hateful sun had been traded for a milder sibling. He fingered the jacket across his lap, the briefcase close at hand, the warm ring on his finger. He had reclaimed it from Dan only after the water had cooled and puddled on the floorboards.

The salesman had found the mattress lumpy and lonely. He had wanted to slip with Dan under the muslin sheets and fall asleep together, but Dan had given him a sad look while blotting the spilled water from the tub.

The familiar sound of his sedan came down the road. He stood up, feeling the years in his lower back and knees. He turned back to the farmhouse, but the only face in the window belonged to the girl.

On the walk between bathroom and bedroom last night, the salesman had passed an open door. By the weak light from the room's window, he had glimpsed the farmer's daughter sitting up in bed, one hand toying with the strings at the front of her nightgown.

The salesman had rested a hand on the doorknob. She lifted and pulled one string taut, revealing more of her chest. He shut her door.

The salesman promised himself to schedule another visit soon on the same route. Perhaps before summer's end. He glanced around at the surrounding fields and raised a hand in farewell for Dan, wherever he might be.

The farmer's son wondered often if the rest of the world might be as magical as the well. Or had he found the only spot on Earth. Both ideas scared him.

The Home Office felt like anything but home. Too many desks filled with secretaries typing, chatting, and trying to catch everyone's eye. Too many rooms filled by other salesmen boasting, laughing, and trying to surpass the next guy's numbers. Water coolers gurgled.

The salesman sat by the far end of the conference room's table. During his years with Link & Grant, he had moved closer to where the CEO sat, before plunging back down to the bottom to sit besides some wiry rookie who sweated over Delaware's routes.

The salesman rubbed at his temples, wishing away the terrible headache that had begun after lunch. Along with a few of the other old-timers, he had gone to a steakhouse and shared cuts of red beef and tumblers of amber whiskey.

His hand shook when he dropped a cube of pure white sugar into his cup. He watched it bob up and down in the miniature black sea as the CEO droned on and on about the price of copper. The immersed cube remained sharp-edged, stained but intact. With a tiny spoon, the salesman stabbed at the sugar, but it refused to dissolve. When he took a sip, he crushed it between his teeth. The taste made him feel worse.

His throat began to ache and he loosened his tie.

Minutes later, he disrupted the meeting by rising and leaving the room quickly with a muttered excuse.

Every employee had a key to the bathroom, a showcase for the company. Each sink and faucet and toilet was different from the next: rows of gleaming brass and stainless steel and old bronze over porcelain bowls.

Out of habit, the salesman went to the farthest, which featured a gilded tap shaped like a swan's neck. He turned the spigot to create a strong flow. His reflection looked pale, his eyes watery.

He splashed cold water onto his face, his neck. He drank from cupped hands. The wet ring on his finger glittered.

When he looked up at the mirror, he saw he was not alone in the bathroom. It took him a moment to recognize the farmer's daughter standing in the shadows of the stalls.

"You're like all the others. Come a callin' but never pay me no mind."

The salesman turned around. He stared at the row of empty toilets. He spun back and in the mirror she stood behind him. Her reflection clutched the back of his neck; he could feel icy hands thrust his head down into the sink's basin.

The salesman closed his eyes to the water, so cold it numbed the pain of striking the porcelain. She shoved his face through the slender drain, the pressure of the pipes mashing his cheekbones, his chin. Then he broke loose at the neck, felt buoyant and relieved, and the stream of water carried him off.

The farmer's son came to the well that afternoon and saw the shiny ring sitting atop the crumbling mortar. He knew before even looking that his sister had added another head. He picked up the ring and leaned over the side. The surface was dark; the heads hid whenever she came by. Tearful, he called out to them, cajoling each to rise up. The salesman's head with its gray hair swirling in the water moved near and allowed him to pet it. The farmer's son would have gladly traded the ring, the sun, anything to kiss a pair of lips a second time.

AUTHOR'S NOTE

THREE YEARS AFTER *Mike's death, I spotted his double in the local newspaper. If my father had not accidentally tossed me the sports section instead of the arts and leisure, I'd never have seen him. I took the paper up to my bedroom and studied the words, but mostly, the photograph. This high school wrestler from Paulsboro had the same block-shaped head, rounded at the ends, the flat nose that I knew to have the same isosceles nostrils as Mike.*

Who was this Matt Suter? He could have been Mike's little brother.

I cut out the article.

Subsequently, I'd read the sports pages hoping to find some mention of Matt. My hunt was an easy one; he was a star athlete, the best in the region, and often mentioned, often pictured. I kept the clippings in a secret folder deep in my closet.

I'd daydream about him. At times he had Mike's laugh, shared Mike's weakness for alcohol. Bitter memories returned. I wondered if Matt slapped his girlfriends around as Mike had done. Wanton memories returned, the times when I'd happened on Mike undressing; I wondered what Matt might look like stripped bare.

Then I happened on Matt's name in the South Jersey section of the paper. What they refer to as a "human interest" piece: the noted wrestler's father had been in a work-related accident and his ailing health was a burden on the family's finances. An address for donations was mentioned at the end.

I wasn't working at the time. I had little money to spare. But I could not resist the chance at some contact with Matt, even one so remote. More money is given to the poor and less fortunate through the patronage of lust than altruism. So I sent off a check, more than I could afford, along with a letter that told the story of how I'd had a college roommate, Mike, who'd wrestled in high school. How Mike came from a broken home and had been lost to drunk driving. That Matt's determination reminded me of him.

The following week brought a letter addressed to me. I tore open the envelope. Inside, a much-folded piece of floral stationery covered in graceful pen strokes. Matt's mother expressed her gratitude for my generosity and wrote how touched she'd been by what had happened to my friend. She encouraged me to attend one of Matt's wrestling matches and say hello.

With an invitation, I couldn't stop myself from seeing him. Even if meant driving hours.

Even from the bleachers of the high school gym, I could smell the mats on the floorboards. Stale and acidic thanks to countless seasons of sweat, blood and vomit. I hid among parents and students. I was thrilled that I could be a voyeur among so many but then bothered by the notion that other men, women, might be there for the same reason.

And so when the boys came out on the floor and they played with the zippers of their jackets, and they began stripping down to their Lycra singlets, I was torn between watching the revelation of so skin and muscle and trying to spy any wickedness in the crowd. And I invented stories. That woman, there, was a housewife who fondled her wine glass as she watched one of the boys mow her lawn. Or the thick-necked guy cheering, he became a sports dad who shivered with repressed desire as he embraced his son after a win. The stories made me feel innocent by comparison.

Matt sat on the Paulsboro bench. He lacked Mike's height by several inches and looked leaner, but now and then I could see him watch the boys on the mat with an intensity that I recognized in Mike years ago. My leg trembled as I watched him. I worried that night I'd have bad dreams about Mike or Matt, or worse, both of them mocking me.

When Matt was called to wrestle, I memorized what I could of his physique as he stood and walked to the center mat. The expansive spread of his chest, the promise of his thighs and ass. His face transformed into a cruel mask and I shook and moaned softly. I'd seen Mike stare down at me with that same expression, the confidence and promise of swift pain and defeat.

Matt stood opposite his opponent, but before the referee allowed them to begin, the announcer leaned into the microphone and recounted the father's accident and urged the audience to donate. Matt's teammates left the bench and spread through the bleachers to collect money in glass jars.

The nearest wrestler possessed a Norman Rockwell face, complete with gap-toothed smile, and sinewy limbs. Traits that would one day bring him fame in amateur porn. I wanted to slip money beneath the straps of his singlet. But he shook the jar at me.

I never could refuse wishing wells, how could I refuse him?

Yes, you were wondering if this Author Note might ever veer near the preceding story. Wishing wells. I adore them. Even the thought of buying a wish for a penny or nickel leaves me breathless. Of course, the thrill is so short-lived. The wishes never come to pass. Einstein would have thought me insane because I can never pass any pool that has glittering coins at the bottom without adding one of my own and hoping that once, just once, my deepest wishes will be granted.

And as I took a twenty dollar bill out of my wallet, the wrestler's thin eyebrows lifted, and his eyes widened at what he no doubt thought was insane generosity. And the thrill that comes over me whenever I toss a coin into the water returned when I dropped the bill into the jar and heard him stammer, Thanks.

I made my wish.

No, it did not involve the wrestler with the jar, though I would encounter him years later.

I ached watching Matt, standing there, restless to begin his match. I left as the referee signaled and Matt hurled himself at his opponent. I could not bear to see if my wish would be granted. Mike would always brood if he ever failed at anything: a dark sulk accentuated by violence and drinking. I listened to him curse as he punched and kicked holes in doors and walls, break things. Some occasions, I wondered which of us was more broken. And though I'm the one still alive, I can't be sure if I'm the one who emerged the least scathed.

After that night, I stopped searching the sports page for mention of Matt. The clippings went to the back of a file cabinet; only on the occasion of writing this did I retrieve the folder, some fifteen years later. Whatever *obsession I'd once felt while looking at his pictures had left me. But I don't dare open up the old album where I kept photographs of Mike.*

Matt would be thirty-three now. As I type this, I imagine him living in suburbia not far away, happily married, a proud father. Maybe one night, he'll pause while climbing the staircase and listen to how quiet his house is and feel the contentment that Mike chased but, in the end, denied himself.

If my wish has been granted.

CAUGHT BY SKIN

SHAWN LINGERS WITH the other 8.34s not far from one of Pe^e/^{a}l's neon-accented bars. A couple of 5.35s—spiky brown hair, cupid lips and deep dimples—pass by, their fingers slipped into each other's pockets. Shawn knows his gaggle envies how fresh they are, but he doesn't feel so much yesteryear-worn as reminded of the hurt. He wonders if any of them have even noticed that Nate is no longer among the gaggle.

New faces were Shawn and Nate's graduation gifts, saved up from dealing and odd jobs. They both agreed on 8.34, advertised in all the e-mags as *East Coast Surf'd* because the original was found and pix'd surfing the artificial beach at Egg Harbor. The clinic was crowded, as if every untouched fag under twenty-five had decided to cash out on having tight blond curls, a button nose, and long lashes lapping aqua eyes. A few old-timers sat on the uncomfortable chairs; one man in maybe his forties whispered excitement at getting his face redone, but his chattiness betrayed the apprehension. Surgery at his age is insane.

Young lifts always refer to his sort as masques. Shawn sees them hover in the corners of the club. They avoid the mirrors on every wall. Nate always tormented them with massive faux-flirting. At the time, Shawn laughed but lately he thinks he was treated the same.

Shawn sips at his stemmed glass. The blend of pure H_2O and flavored spirits is overpriced and over-sweetened with faux berries. The gilding on his credID has recently been replaced and the way the bartender offhandedly swipes it makes him worry that it will be worn away before he is drunk. The bartender is a 2.32. Shawn never likes the February faces with their rosy cheeks—as if it has snowed in Jersey since '29.

He wants distraction, anything to divert his thoughts from Nate. A few months back, he thought he heard Nate's laugh, mocking and high and ending with that telling sucked-in breath, coming from a 1.35.

Thankfully, he has some Prism. He forgets which one of the gaggle pressed the hollow plastic stick into his palm. He leans back against the bar's metal and neon railing and squirts a hit into each eye.

A tiny bit drips down his cheek and chin. He wipes his face with his fingers and blinks as his vision changes. He doesn't really understand how the drug affects the rods or cones or whatever in his eyes, limiting the spectrum to one color—orange this time. But what matters to him is the euphoria, never as much as promised these days, but then he's been taking Prism since fifteen.

The Pe^e/^{a}l is hot from all the bodies, as everyone clusters together. Gaggledom. Shawn tugs at his shirt's wide collar, decorated with his birthstones. The synthetics of his top and flared shorts are totally non-absorbent so alcohol and sweat and come roll off them; by the end of the evening Shawn will be slick under his clothes. The natural-fiber skivs would be drenched, so he doesn't wear any while clubbing.

As a sense of buoyancy eases over him, he smirks at the notion of falling out of sync and making out with a different lift; the other 8.34s would hate him. Twinning is everything. He remembers fucking Nate and discovering only afterwards that it wasn't really his best friend but another of the gaggle. But that will not happen again. He halfheartedly curses Nate for abandoning him for May's look but then music starts leaking through the speaker tiles on the dance floor at the other side of the bar and Shawn tries and fails to recognize the stylist. Probably an invent by some clubber in New Delhi with not enough sleep and plenty of meds, he decides. Bollypopper. A few of the illuminated tiles start rising and falling, like the Atlantic, cresting on the beat. Dancing requires attention or genetics, and Shawn knows that he has to wait a half hour after Prism before daring the dance floor or else look freaked.

The nearest 8.34, skin more pumpkin than tan thanks to the Prism, nudges his arm to share his drink and Shawn tries to remember if his name is Ragan...or maybe it's Fox—which one wears the liquid crystal necklace flashing *PwrBttm?* He hands the glass over and in two sips it's empty. Fox then. Another 8.34 laughs at Shawn and the rest of the gaggle follows suit. Most, he knows, have no idea why they laugh and only mimic the rest.

Disgusted, he walks away from them towards the bathroom. As he nears the doorway, a masque reaches out for him. "I love Augusts." The lips are stretched so tight around a 3.35 jawline a hiss escapes with each word.

Shawn escapes and heads towards the front doors, wanting whatever passes for Jersey fresh air. The bouncer, gruff and untouched by surgery, argues with a guy in the doorway. Shawn stops when his ocherous vision takes in how striking the guy is. The face is not any lift he's seen before. Instinctively, he reaches for his I-Point. He needs a moment to focus the tiny screen, before capturing with a retro click-sound the shiny dark hair, parted down the center, a slightly upturned nose, and eyes such a pale orange that Shawn figures they must be gray.

The bouncer refuses to allow the guy inside. Once Shawn has sent the natural's image out to the GillienNet with a push of a button, he walks over.

"Debut, here, has no cred." The bouncer has tattoos along his cheeks that resemble tusks. Shawn heard that the Pe^e/^{a}l's owners wouldn't have any lifts work the door. Pretties and drags get lifts, the roughs want ink, especially teethmarks.

"I'm new around here," the natural says with a slight shrug.

Shawn holds out his credID to the bouncer who swipes it over the pad on the wall. "Easy. Now you're mine for the evening." Shawn's joking but the natural responds with such a wide grin that Shawn cannot help but smile back.

"What's your name?"

"Shawn."

"That's it?" The guy's thick eyebrows rise. "No number? I thought with clones—"

"Clones?" Shawn huffs air around a slight laugh. "Does this look Third World?" he asks, stepping back and motioning his hands up and down his face and body. But the sting of the insult fades fast as Shawn realizes a natural would have no idea how much can be spent on matching a month. They are almost another species.

"No. Sorry." The guy looks embarrassed. "Just all the similar faces."

Shawn steps so close to the guy that he could kiss him. Instead he examines the face with as much attention as the Prism allows. He sees no scars, no telltale signs of surgery. The earlobes are attached, but then so were the faces of two years ago. Slight creases along the edges of the eyes suggest age. Maybe he's S-prone, Schizo. "You just wake up and find you're 21st cent?"

"Something like that." The natural looks down at himself, as if noticing he's wearing clothes for the first time.

Shawn finds himself curious. It feels like ages since his lift and he doesn't remember the last time he said more than a few words to a natural in passing. He takes the guy's hand in his own and pulls him towards the nearest bar. "Drink time."

Flashes staccato the air as other guys start pixing the stranger's face. They all wish to be the first to upload his features to the GillienNet in the hopes they will find June or July's face and earn a free lift.

The bartender swipes more of Shawn's money away. The aquahol is cold. The stranger sips his cautiously and seems not to know where to look: at the thin glass holding his drink, at the bar, or back at Shawn.

"So how about a name?" Shawn taps glasses.

"I wish I could offer one. Well, other than the Student."

"A u-boy?" None of the gaggle is into education. Degrees are for expired lifts and masques.

"I don't even know what that is."

"As in university."

"Once. Maybe. At least, I think so. They rationed our long-term memory to reduce culture shock."

"They?"

The Student lightly rubs at his temples. "That I can't recall."

Definitely schizo, thinks Shawn. But far better than the same chatter from the same mouths. "So this means you're from…?"

"The future. Or maybe the past."

"Like vids?" Shawn waves for a refill. He never expects to have to think while talking with a guy. But he finds himself enjoying the novelty of chatting with a schizo natural. The orange tint of the world is wearing off.

"No. I'm never sure how long I have somewhen. And there's pain."

"Oh?" The bartender hands over another glass.

"SHC."

"Lost me."

"Spontaneous human combustion. The energy needed to transmit matter—sorry, this must sound insane."

Shawn grins. "But not boring." He tries to remember what sort of conversations he had with Nate but he cannot recall any, either pre-lift or as part of the gaggle. The void leaves him all mawks, worsening the descent from the Prism. He needs to chase away regrets, so he slides a hand up the Student's arm and leans forward. His kiss is met.

"Your peer group…your fellows are watching us."

Shawn turns around and sees the gaggle staring and whispering.

"Perhaps we should go someplace else? You could tell me more—"

Shawn gulps his entire drink. "Let's go upstairs?" If the gaggle plans on passing judgment on him, he might as well be truly guilty.

The Student's eyebrows raise as he glances at the ceiling. "What's upstairs?"

"C'mon," Shawn says and tugs on the Student's arm.

More flashes erupt as they wend their way past the dance floor. Shawn tries to block their pix out of a blend of ownership and some sense of protecting his catch. At one point, the Student nearly trips on a raised tile, and Shawn catches him. More kissing happens as a result of the rescue.

The escalator up is a quaint old ride, one slow enough that clubbers can see who exactly is going upstairs with whom. Shawn leans over the moving black rail and catches the gaggle of 8.34s gawking at him, their identical expressions showing alarm at his decision. He feels a schizo-like rush and leers down at them, while sliding a hand up the Student's shirtfront. When his fingers discover thick chest hair it's such a shock that he almost stumbles off the step. He recovers with an embarrassed half-smile.

The top floor of Pe^e/^{a}l is far dimmer than the rest. Shawn guides the Student through the antechamber with its padded lining. Couples and trines relax against the soft walls in the endorphin-slake. The Student requires further tugging to move past them all.

"So why all the same faces?"

"Hmm?" Shawn hands over his credID to secure a booth. Shawn nods to the attendant, a poorly done 1.35 who has failed to cover the scar-traces along his temples with concealer.

"Obviously ageism, but the conduct norms of embracing societal-wide total cosmetic surgery as a conscience collective is fascinating."

Shawn laughs at the Student. "Because we all want to be young, if only on the outside." Then he stops laughing. The aquahol must have been shit because he feels suddenly mawks. "But it's all a trap. Your insides get older and older and end up wanting something else but by then you're caught by skin." Shawn thinks of Nate leaving him for the 5.35s.

They walk down hall lined with booths. Groans and moans slip past shut doors.

The Student reaches out and lightly strokes his face. He leans into the touch. "But if you can change your looks often, why ever feel trapped?" A thumb brushes against his lips, which instinctively part for a moment.

"How long can you chase faces?" He envisions Nate a month or two from now getting yet another lift, trying to stay with the now.

"Imagine chasing entire cultures, never sure how long you'll be anyplace, anytime." The Student frowns then looks away. "I'm so anxious over burning off before I really assess the period's norms that I end up with hasty examinations, desperate for any sampling."

"Desperate?"

The Student nods.

From one of the nearby booths comes a heavy smack against the door. Both are startled and jump from the sudden sound. They laugh too.

"Any sampling?" asks Shawn. The anticipation of play with the Student chases away some of the mawks.

"Well, some studies are more rewarding than others." The Student offers an embarrassed grin. "How different from where I was last," he says. "They're all so very different, though."

"Where...I mean, when was the last...time?" Shawn doesn't believe the guy, but talking crazy has to be better than conceding how miserable he is.

"*Yìhétuán Qi yì.*" The tonal inflection is perfect, showing years of study on the mainland.

"*Che ji ba dan!*" Shawn playfully pushes the Student on the chest, knocking him into the padded wall.

"You speak Chinese?"

"Doesn't half the world these days?" Shawn moves closer, brushing his mouth against the Student's ear. "Chinese history was my fav in school." He can't resist lightly licking the Student's neck. He tastes the salty tang of sweat. "I can't imagine you as a Boxer."

"*Yìhétuán,*" whispers the Student. He presses his hand against the back of Shawn's head.

"Fisting is illegal these days...or should be." Shawn playfully bites an earlobe.

"That's *Yìhéquán.*" He moans slightly. "You brought me up here to *gan*, right?"

Shawn nods and leads the Student to an empty booth. He shuts the door.

Along one wall are bins. Shawn begins stripping off his clothes. The Student watches a moment before following suit. Shawn stares at his body with its natural musculature, the amount of fat in spots along the midsection, the swathe of hair along the chest and stomach. He feels awkward, naked, with his size-2 pectoral implants and the results of his latest abdominal-sculpting visit. Comparing himself to the Student, Shawn feels manufactured, artificial and, for the first time in almost a year, ugly.

Ashamed, he turns away, busying himself with stowing their clothes in the bins. He then presses the first button on the wall.

A fine mist descends. The Student raises both hands, palms up, to catch the drops. Shawn marvels at the sight, for if the guy isn't schizo—if he could even be what he claims—he's totally unafraid of anything new.

"This is?"

"Disinfectant." Shawn starts rubbing the dew from the mist over his body and then helps the Student. His hands roam all over before focusing on the thick chode rapidly hardening. He realizes the Student is curiously disfigured down there, lacking the silky skin everyone else possesses, but Shawn says nothing, not wanting to embarrass him.

"No aftertaste?" The Student kisses him hard before bringing his lips down Shawn's chin and neck. "Thankfully, no," he says and starts licking Shawn's chest.

They each touch and taste the other's torso a while, before taking turns on their knees. Shawn hesitates before taking the flawed chode into his mouth. His fingers rub the reddened tip where the extra skin should hang. Thick coarse hair surrounds the chode and even the disinfectant has not chased away the pungent but not unpleasant smell. He treats it tenderly in his mouth in case the Student's disfigurement has left him sensitive. The response he earns is soft groans and encouraging strokes back and forth through his lips.

Eventually, Shawn is so eager to be had that he rises and presses his face and chest against the cool wall. He pushes back with his hips, spreading slightly his legs. He aches to have the Student crush against him. "Please," he begs.

Shawn feels the warm breath against his back and the touch of the hot chode against one cheek. Then the Student's fingers are parting his ass. It's a sensation he's often been curious of, but never dared.

"What are you doing?" Shawn asks, his voice rising slightly, nervous.

"What's natural," the Student replies and a fingertip tries to force its way inside.

"No, what are you doing?" Shawn nearly shouts. He turns around to see the Student standing there, looking shocked.

"I-I thought you wanted me to fuck you."

"No one does ass anymore." He takes a deep breath and relaxes. He slides a hand around the Student's neck. "I take it you're not aware of Bleeds? It's not safe." Sean kisses him as a makeshift apology. Then he takes hold of the Student's chode, strokes it hard once more. "Here," he says, slowly turns back to the wall, then guiding the hot shaft between his thighs. "Like this." He clenches his legs shut, not too tight, but locked so they firmly rub against the Student.

"Oh. Oh. Intercrural? I haven't done this since...Sophocles?" The Student, with apparent skill at the technique, wraps his arms around Shawn, one hand down so both their chodes are rubbed. He begins kissing the back of Shawn's neck and achieving the perfect rhythm.

Shawn feels the pressure rise within him. He cries out as he sprays the plastic walls. The Student takes longer, but soon he coats Shawn's legs. They stand still, together, for a while, until they no longer gasp.

The Student presses the shower button and another mist falls on them, rinsing off the sweat and semen. Their clothes, protected by the bin, are dry.

"So, what now?" the Student asks.

Shawn has no ready answer. He adjusts his clothes, feels the meaninglessness of the gesture. With Nate, with even the other 8.34s, he always knew what would happen next, but a natural poses so many mysteries, especially one with wild claims.

He glances at his I-Point's tiny display. Hours to go before the gaggle will leave Peᵉ/ᵃl; he needs to stay late enough not to encounter any of them awake in the suite. He hopes they won't be so vengeful they lock him out.

"Hmmm. I'm short on cred. How about I show you how we dance here?"

The Student laughs. "I have to warn you, no matter what the year, I'm a really bad dancer."

==

THE GAGGLE PUNISHES Shawn for straying, making him stay inside their collective apartments. It's five nights later, he can return to Peᵉ/ᵃl. During his exile, he waited for a message from the Student. None came. Distraught, Shawn's not sure whether the natural might have been telling the truth and has no idea how to message, or is just S-prone and doesn't want to. Neither thought is comforting or lessens the daydreams about the Student. He searches the club, wandering the place. When he finally does spot the face that has preoccupied the last hundred twenty hrs, he's surprised to see the Student out on the dance floor. For a professed bad dancer, he has mastered the latest spin.

Shawn rushes over to him and touches his shoulder fondly. The Student looks at him without any trace of recognition before returning to dancing. Shawn blinks in surprise and frustration and pushes the Student, knocking him from finishing the twirl.

"So, what, your memory getting worse?"

"Like I hang with August trash." The voice is wrong. So wrong. High-pitched. The surgeons never dare the vocal cords for fear of litigation.

Shawn stumbles back. He bumps into someone and turns around to apologize and sees it's another Student. The guy scowls, transforming the handsome features into something horrid. A bad job, too tight around the jawline.

Shawn rushes out of the heaving dance floor. He makes it to the front door in time to see two more Students walking in. He pushes past them. Outside, the air is hot and stagnant. June weather in NJ. His I-Point shivers. Instinctively, he runs his fingertips over the controls and checks his messages.

GillienNetAdmin
Congratulations, Shawn Carte, you are the primary sender of 6.35's chosen visage. To accept your complimentary facial surgery, please stop in at your approved clinic and present this code.

Beneath the message is the picture he took, transmitted and forgotten, of the Student by the club's entrance.

He looks back at the club entrance. Shawn knows that every night will bring more of the Student's face. Maybe even Nate will walk through the door, eager to show off the latest lift. But Shawn would never be able to find him—or the real Student—not amongst the next month's gaggle.

He almost deletes the message. Then he glances at the tiny screen capture of the Student's face, imagining Nate behind it, kissing those lips and hearing once more his best friend's soft murmurs of delight. Shawn finds himself looking at past pix, the oldest files, with Nate's and his original faces. He taps the panel and zooms and aches for the past.

Halfway to the rail station, he finds through the GillienNet a decent clinic still open. Shawn isn't sure that he can trade his complimentary lift. Impatient, he paces the platform. The other passengers—all naturals but a pair of girls who are on the verge of twinning, combing hands through ringlets of copper hair and ruddy lips, pressing each other against the map monitor—give him wary glances.

A warm gust heralds the car's arrival. In the few seconds after the rail stops, he sees in the mirrored door panels not his own reflection but Nate's virgin face. Shawn thinks he will wear it well.

AUTHOR'S NOTE

I've always thought that good science fiction needs to be daring. Being timid, I'd never written any such story before. Then Cecilia Tan asked me for a story. I almost refused but then, after a night out on the town with my gaggle, I became inspired. And while I can't recall all that happened that night, I hope this captures some of that evening's splendor:

OUR CAST

THE BRAIN, *a supervillain from DC Comics (we met during the Portentous Crisis limited series when I was an assistant editor)*

ME, *circa 2005*

ROBOT, *from* Lost in Space *television series (we met at Nova Newark 4, a fandom convention)*

SINGER, *from the novel* Deathgift *(our first date was following an alien abduction)*

VENOMU, *assassin from* Guilty Gear *video games (we met in the backroom of Balls N Pockets, a gay pool hall)*

SCENE

(Woody's, a nightclub in downtown Philadelphia. Attractive men wander the dimly lit stage. THE BRAIN, the mind of an evil genius floating in a mobile jar, STEVE, a hapless author in his mid-30s, the antiquated ROBOT, sit around a table not far from the bar. Their friend VENOMU, a bare-chested assassin with long hair in his eyes, plays pool by himself in the adjoining room.)

STEVE

And then I said, "That's the second biggest coprolite I've ever seen."

(He gestures wide with extended arms.)

ROBOT
(ROBOT laughs. In one extendable arm it clutches a plastic quart of motor oil decorated with a tiny umbrella.)

THE BRAIN
(He sighs dramatically)

I wonder if he misses me.

STEVE

Mallah's only been gone two days. He's still probably haggling over yellowcake with the North Koreans.

ROBOT

That's enriched.

VENOMU

I once killed eight men in a Korean massage parlor.

(He stabs at the air with a pool cue.)

STEVE

I wanted one night, one relaxing night.

THE BRAIN

I hate this place. Last time I went into the bathroom, some meth'd twink thought I was a prophylactic dispenser. He kept trying to shove a quarter into my data port.

VENOMU

Why would a brain in a jar need to use the bathroom?
STEVE and ROBOT
(STEVE and ROBOT turn to regard one another.)
Tea roomin'!

THE BRAIN

N-no.

(His gray matter flushes pink)

I was...I was just going to freshen up.

(A handsome man walks past the table. THE BRAIN pivots.)

Look at the ass on that guy.

(REST OF CAST turns to admire the guy. In doing so, VENOMU scratches the cue ball and curses.)

If I had an ass like that... I could rule the world.

VENOMU

The world?

THE BRAIN
Well maybe just this bar.

ROBOT
(Pours some motor oil over THE BRAIN)

THE BRAIN
That better be 25 W.

(Music begins to play—the opening theme to
Flash Gordon by Queen.)

THE BRAIN
This song... When I was a boy, I had the biggest crush
on Hans Zarkov. I'd daydream about that rocket of
his. He's the reason I became a mad scientist.

STEVE
This song... When I was fifteen, my oldest sister figured
out that I'd been looking through her room and reading
her diary. A couple days later, as she's leaving the
house, she tells me to stop burgling and that there's an
issue of Playboy under her bed.

So I'm home alone. So, I go into her room and reach
under her bed for the magazine. It wasn't a Playboy,
though but a Playgirl.

VENOMU
So she knew?

STEVE
Maybe. Maybe it was a bribe to leave her stuff alone.

(STEVE looks offstage and drinks)

She doesn't remember any of this now. But I'll never forget. Those glossy pages. They could barely contain all the muscles and hair.

You never forget the first photograph you fall in lust after. A young Sam Jones. He was Flash Gordon, my Flash Gordon. So beautiful, feigning sleep on a poolside chair while the sun kissed him tan. My eyes wanted to take in the whole but could never do so. They'd flicker to his face, then that chest, the thick clot of pubes, his dick.

My Flash Gordon.

(STEVE rubs at his face as if wiping it clean. Then he looks over the other men in the bar.)

They're all so much prettier than me.

(He stirs his glass, empty but for ice.)

VENOMU
The Yakuza have surgeons that can give you any face you want.

THE BRAIN
Something more simian would be nice.

STEVE
Boys on paper are so much safer. Paper cuts are better than broken hearts.

(Cast grows quiet for a couple of minutes.)

THE ROBOT
Danger, Steve Berman, danger.

(ROBOT points with one clawed arm STAGE
LEFT, presumably Woody's front door.)

Your ex just walked in.

(Enter SINGER, a lean, tall guy, handsome, with a
scar across the left side of his face.)

STEVE
(He looks at SINGER, then groans)
He's back to sporting the scar.

(He turns around in his seat, trying to hide from view)

VENOMU
Scars are sexy. Especially if they lead somewhere.

THE ROBOT
(Spins chassis around.)
Earned these scratches at the Deadly Games of Gamma 6.

THE BRAIN
Liar. You told me they're from when Major West made
you his bitch.

VENOMU
Here he comes.

STEVE
He never gives up.

THE BRAIN
I think he's reading my mind.

(His mobile jar trembles.)

All my schemes, my beautiful schemes.

ROBOT
All your schematics, your crappy schematics.

SINGER
(*SINGER walks over to the table.*)
Hey. You look good.

VENOMU
(*He walks over and stands protectively behind*
STEVE.)

He's planning on having his face changed.

STEVE

Am not.
SINGER
I hope not. Would be a shame.

(*He looks uncomfortably around the others.*)

Look, can we go someplace and talk?

STEVE
(*He finishes off his drink.*)
Why, so you can sweet talk me again?

(*He shakes his head.*)

You'll just go all distant and jump off-world on me
again.

(*SINGER rests a hand on STEVE's shoulder.*
VENOMU menaces with the pool cue.)

SINGER
It was only to visit my sick mother in Alpha Centauri.
That's barely a parsec away.

ROBOT
(ROBOT emits a deep guttural laugh.)
Heard that one before.

(ROBOT high-fives VENOMU and THE BRAIN,
who obviously leaves the ROBOT hanging.)

STEVE
You could have signaled.

SINGER
My sub-space was down, hon.

(SINGER runs a hand over STEVE's cheek.)

I missed this face.

(STEVE leans into his touch.)

STEVE
(He pushes back his chair.)
I guess we could talk.

THE BRAIN
I thought we were here to cheer me up.

ROBOT
(Taps THE BRAIN's jar with his claw.)
It's always about you.

STEVE
(Stands up. He proceeds to hug each of his friends.
He whispers to THE BRAIN:)
He's lying, but I need to be wanted again, to feel before
the hurt again.

(He then leaves with SINGER.)

THE BRAIN
Great, just great. Mallah's miles and miles away, Steve's
off shagging Singer's boots off and I'm stuck with you
two.

VENOMU
What about those little guys at the end of the bar?

(Stage lighting reveals three short figures in brown
robes holding drinks. Their cowls are up and only their
eyes, glowing yellow spots are visible. They speak in an
incoherent high pitch.)

ROBOT
(ROBOT flails his mechanical arms about.)
Danger, danger!

REST OF CAST
Shut up, you ninny!

A ROTTEN OBLIGATION

THE CAR WAS nothing to look at—a battered hunk from some by-now-closed domestic factory, its gray primer dappled with rust spots—but the driver was. Young, thin, with too much dark hair that kept falling into his eyes as he tried to stay awake. He blinked away the latest yawn and swerved back from the edge of the highway he had been drifting towards.

The headlights flashed over a small, faded sign of a fork and knife.

"There's a truck stop ahead."

"So?" Daley's voice came from the empty passenger seat.

Joe turned instinctively at the sound and saw his mentor sitting there smoking a cigarette.

"I need some coffee," Joe said. "Bad. Something to eat too would be nice."

"Shit, you're whining again."

"You drive then."

"Heh." Daley's ghost flipped him the finger. "Finally got a sense of humor. Fine, but let's not spend too long."

After ten miles of silence—the radio had died long before they had set out from Philly—they pulled into the rest stop's parking lot. The neon light from the diner washed over the few sleeping semis and made the blacktop glow orange and yellow.

Joe parked and stretched when he got out of the car. He figured he had been cramped behind the wheel for three hours since the last time they'd stopped for gas and oil. Reaching into his pocket, he pulled out a shrinking wad of bills. There'd be enough to fill up the tank some more—Daley was pathological about not running out of gas and ending up leaving his corpse stranded—and get a little something in his stomach. After that, he'd have to find another horny trucker to blow for cash. He shivered inwardly at the memory of the last time. The grunts, the stink of sweat. Not something he wanted to think about before eating.

Inside, he slipped into a booth, barely glancing at anyone else.

Daley appeared there, opposite him, a moment later. Joe tried not to notice him and stared at the stained menu, scratching off a bit of dried gravy to read what the soup was. Chicken okra. What the hell was an okra?

"Order steak and eggs."

"Fuck off," Joe muttered under his breath. He was getting sick of Daley. To think, Joe had idolized him when the guy had been alive. He'd even wanted him.

"I miss the smell. It'll make me feel better."

Joe glanced over the menu. "You shouldn't have trusted that dealer. Dose o' Drano made you feel real good, right?"

"Just order the fucking steak."

"I don't have enough."

"You can hustle for more."

Joe bit back the harsh yell building at the back of his throat, knowing that everyone at the truck stop would think he was totally insane if he started screaming at the empty seat across from him. "Fine."

Daley smiled, a smug grin that had once been his best feature. Thin lips that everyone had wanted to kiss but he didn't let you unless you paid extra. Twenty bucks to share some spit. Lots of guys spent that extra Andrew Jackson.

The waitress came over chewing a mouthful of gum or cud or whatever. She wore more makeup than a whore. Joe knew about whores. "Whatya have, sweetie?"

Joe actually liked being called that. Better than the "boy" or "baby" that he was usually called. He warmed to her, gave her a smile. Daley laughed, hacking on his ectoplasmic unfiltereds.

"Cup of coffee, plenty of refills, the steak and sunny eggs and a side of potatoes."

"Gotcha. Been traveling long?"

He nodded. "Need to reach Arizona."

She sucked in a breath, showing some lipstick on her front teeth. "Long way to go there. I'll make sure there's a fresh pot for you."

The coffee she poured into one of those little ceramic cups you only drink out of in restaurants was better than Joe expected. She must have not lied about the fresh brew. He poured in a healthy dose of sugar and ignored the little tubs of half-and-half. When he was a kid, he'd loved to play with them, his fingers lightly squeezing, trying to press his luck to the point where the creamers were on the edge of bursting. Then his father would yell at him, smacking him on the shoulder, and he'd stop. He'd never purposefully opened one.

Soon the waitress returned with two plates, one big and bearing the browned steak and two orange eyes staring from a white face, the other small and heaped with breakfast potatoes.

"Ahh," Daley said, leaning over the large plate and sniffing so loudly that Joe was disgusted.

The steak looked barely edible. It was thin—maybe the cow had been anorexic—with little fat, more like a piece of hide. Daley continued sniffing as Joe started to cut into the steak. It took him a while to carve out a small piece. The cow had definitely had some disorder to end up like this.

Joe didn't care for steak. Never liked meat that much. But hustlers couldn't be that choosey. A full stomach was such a rarity. There had been one guy who stopped when he saw Joe sitting on the corner and started talking. The usual thing, what are you up to and all that. That was one of the things Joe hated about hustling, the bullshit. Daley loved it, told him time and time again what to say, like it was a game, which it truly was. Only Daley seemed to think that the johns were the losers and Joe had decided he wasn't so sure.

Anyway, the guy asked him when he had eaten last and immediately Joe thought this was gonna turn out wrong, maybe with a dollar or something like he was a beggar instead of a whore. But no, the guy treated him to some fast food around the corner, and then they had gone back to the guy's apartment and kissed and the greasy stink of the hamburgers was over the man's breath and Joe had ended up in the bathroom throwing up and leaving without so much as a dime.

He took one last look at the meat and then popped it into his mouth. It chewed like leather. The coffee helped it down.

"Damn, I wish I could have a bite."

Joe shrugged. Why bother telling him how awful it really was? Daley never really listened to him. Just told him what to do. He dug into the eggs, shaking his head lightly and angry with himself for ending up where he was.

Dumb to run away from home. Dumb to end up on the street hustling. Doubly dumb to latch onto Daley, who was just looking for someone to mentor, to dispense a jaded perception of the world. And just so fucking dumb to listen to a dead man's request to be buried where it's warm.

Daley meanwhile had been looking around the truck stop. "The busboy's been staring at you."

"What?"

Daley nodded over his shoulder. He might as well have walked over to where the guy was and hollered and done jumping-jacks; he still would have gone unseen.

Joe did catch a glance from the busboy, who immediately looked back from his work clearing a nearby table. The young guy was the opposite of Joe, blond, weighed more than a hundred and twenty, and looked good. Well, the last was a lie, Joe knew guys and girls found him cute, but he had begun to hate how little-boyish he had become. Small face, little body. He looked sixteen. He could drink legally if he had a license.

While he was staring at the busboy, the guy looked back and gave a slight smile. Inwardly, Joe wasn't sure if he should be groaning or not. Flirting didn't seem the right thing to do, not when he was strung out from too little sleep and trying to get a dead body across the country. He rubbed his temples idly. Still, the guy was majorly cute.

He finished his third cup of steaming black coffee, the eggs and most of the potatoes. The steak remained on the plate, except for the small portion he had endeavored to stomach.

The waitress tore off his check and left it with a smile and a pat on the shoulders. He went to the register to pay, then back to the counter to leave the tip. The busboy was cleaning up. Daley still sat there, grinning and making lewd faces at the guy.

Joe left more than a generous tip. He left everything he had, which wasn't much.

The busboy looked up at him with that same slight smile as he picked up the plate with the remaining steak. "Didn't like it?"

"I'm not a big carnivore."

"Then why'd you order it?"

"Go on," laughed Daley. "Tell him."

"Smelled good."

"Pussy," Daley said, stubbing out his cigarette in the ashtray. Nothing was left behind.

The busboy laughed. "That's the first time I heard that."

"So," Joe started, unsure where he was heading. "What's there to do around here?"

"Here? Nothing. We're one exit from Nowhere and down the road from Dullsville."

Joe nodded. Daley urged him to bring the boy back to the car, fuck him, and then steal his wallet.

"Passing through?"

"Yeah, well, I'm on an errand for a friend but...well, I guess I have some time."

"Really?" The busboy bit his lower lip. It was a cute gesture.

Unfortunately Joe responded with a sudden yawn.

"You must be tired."

"Yeah, been driving all night."

"Well, if you need someplace to crash for a night—"

Daley barked a laugh. "Little faggot wants your ass, Joe."

Joe took a step closer. "I was planning on sleeping in the car."

"Nah, that's no good. I have a sofa."

Joe looked at the guy's face but saw none of the usual awful guile and lust he saw in men. He was tired, he told himself. A few hours rest someplace decent might not be such a bad idea. Daley wouldn't be any deader. The trunk of his car would just be a little nastier.

"Okay."

"What the fuck are you doing?" Daley came close to Joe's ear, practically shouting.

Joe ignored the ghost.

"I'm Evan. I'll be done my shift in about twenty minutes."

Sipping water from a glass while Daley fumed over the delay, Joe waited for Evan to finish.

The cute guy slipped a thick coat over his stained white T-shirt. "Do you want to ride along or follow me in your car?"

Joe was sick of driving; he'd like nothing more if it were weeks before he had to get behind the wheel again. All the coffee he had drunk seemed to have passed through him, unnoticed by his fuzzy brain. But leaving the car behind was a no-no. Anyone getting too close might notice something. Like, say, the corpse kept in the trunk.

"I better follow."

Daley continued to mouth off on the drive to Evan's place. Joe drove with the window open, letting cold air blow in his face, numbing him to everything, yet keeping him awake.

"Nothing special, but it's home." Evan turned on the light and stepped aside so that Joe could walk from the cramped stairwell into the small apartment.

"It's nice." Joe had learned how to lie with casual ease, but this time he wasn't. Okay, the place was no mansion, but it was clean, warm, the furniture not pockmarked with cigarette burns or indescribable stains, no overflowing trash. A nice place.

"Thanks."

Joe was about to throw his own jacket on the sofa, when Evan reached out for it, finding it a hanger in the tiny closet. When he shut the door Daley appeared.

"I bet this boy even bakes cookies," he snickered.

"You want to take a shower?"

Joe sniffed at his shoulder. "That bad?"

Evan chuckled. "No, just thought it might relax you."

"Okay."

"The bathroom's this way."

Joe followed after Evan, noticing how the guy's torso looked good underneath the thin cotton shirt.

"Here's a towel for you." When Evan handed over the towel their hands briefly met. Joe suddenly found himself blushing, something he could not recall happening in ages.

"Umm, thanks."

Evan grinned and left Joe alone in the bathroom. Or so he thought. Daley sat on the toilet.

"I'd look in the medicine cabinet."

"I don't think he stocks anything that would help you."

"I was thinking he probably has all these AIDS drugs."

"Fuck off." Joe started to strip off his clothes. It had been too long since he last bathed and his bare skin felt dirty, almost unhealthy. He had just peeled off his boxers, holding them by the frayed waistband and wondering if Evan would let him do some laundry, when Daley spoke up.

"I don't think I ever saw you naked before."

Joe found his dead mentor staring at him. The thought of Daley watching him was very disturbing. He turned around a bit so that his front faced the shower curtain.

"What's that?"

Over his shoulder he saw Daley pointing at his hip. Joe looked down. The pink triangle tattoo on his hip bone, inches above the dark unruly patch of pubic hair, greeted his eyes.

"Something I got before I met you. Wanted to piss off my folks."

Daley shook his head in disgust.

The hot spray of the shower washed away more than a week's worth of grime. His muscles finally relaxed, the sinews and tendons in his arms and back unwound, until by the time he had used up most of the hot water, he was slumped against the tiled wall, panting but happy. He pushed aside the dripping plastic curtain. Daley was gone, but Joe knew that was only for the moment. He dried off and wrapped the towel about his waist. The uppermost section of the triangle was still visible. He piled his clothes into a corner.

Evan was tucking in a sheet into the crevices of the sofa when Joe stepped out. His host opened his mouth to say something but instead swallowed the words and shyly looked down at his feet.

"Drop the towel." Daley stood behind Joe, his voice in his ear. "Watch what happens. Do it."

Joe pulled at his waist and the towel loosened and fell to the floor with a whisper.

Evan looked up, his eyes widening slightly, staring for a moment before traveling up and down Joe's body. He took a few steps closer, until inches separated them.

"Heh, faggots never can resist dick."

Joe held his breath though, feeling weirdly nervous. He had been naked in front of another guy countless times before, but he had never wanted to be touched. It seemed like they would stay still, apart, forever, until Joe could not stand it anymore, and reached out and took hold of Evan's hand and placed it on his own swelling cock.

The guy's grip was gentle, light, the fingertips moving ever so slightly back and forth over the sensitive tip. Joe gasped, shocked at how good it felt. This was how it was supposed to feel, maybe how all the johns felt when he touched them. No, they could never feel this good. His knees felt weak and he fell forward slightly, leaning against the still-dressed Evan, his head resting in the curve of the guy's neck. He murmured words, heard Daley's mocking sounds, but listened only to the heart beating rapidly in the firm chest beneath his hand.

It took only a moment for the rush to begin, travel from Joe's spine to the base of his cock, and then erupt, spraying the legs of Evan's jeans. Joe bucked against Evan but was held tightly, his bare back rubbed down to his small cheeks.

They collapsed down onto the floor near the sofa and began to finally kiss. Joe fell asleep soon after that.

—

Daley's bitching was bad the following day, when Joe spent it at Evan's, worse the day after when Joe promised that he just wanted a little rest and fun before they resumed the trip to Arizona. But come the fourth day, when Joe woke in Evan's bed, smiling at the warmth of the covers and the still-sleeping boy besides him, the maddening complaints from his dead mentor would not cease.

Finally, he pulled on a pair of jeans—his, now freshly laundered—and went down the steps to the outside. The ghost trailed along after him.

"This is fucking bullshit! You promised to help me. Now get your namby ass into that car and let's go!"

Bare-chested, standing on the building's porch, Joe shivered. Winter had only just begun. Still, he needed someplace to talk to Daley, to tell him the truth.

"No."

"No? What's this 'no' shit?" A puff of unreal smoke drifted into Joe's face, causing him to instinctively blink.

"That's just it. No. As in, I'm not going. I want to stay here."

"What, and be Miz Suzie Homemaker with your little boyfriend?"

Joe reached for the doorknob. "He's getting me a job at the diner. See, he's good to me, for me. Why leave?"

Daley went to block him from going upstairs but stopped at the last moment, knowing he truly couldn't. "You promised."

"That was back when I thought I'd only have you." Joe rushed up the steps, eager to return to both the bed and Evan.

Daley did not appear for the rest of the day. Joe doubted that was the end; Daley was just too stubborn to give up so easily. Joe would have to find some way to get rid of the car, maybe abandon it someplace without the tags. Not having the corpse around might help rid him of the ghost.

That night Joe woke suddenly. A sound had disturbed him. He blinked and looked to his right. Evan slumbered away after a grueling double shift at the diner and some labor-intensive fucking.

Again came a dull thud from the front room. Joe slipped out of bed and quietly opened the door. The entire apartment was dark. He shuffled forward, cautiously, more worried that he'd bump into something and wake Evan than about finding a burglar.

"Time to go, Joe."

Daley.

"Ugh, only you." Joe groaned and turned around towards the bedroom.

Then he heard an unmistakable click from behind him and a weak light hit the walls of the apartment. Confused, he looked back. Sitting on the sofa, its face a rictus, was Daley. The real Daley, the one supposed to be in the trunk of the car. He must have gotten out and broken in. A moldering hand was still on the switch of the small tableside lamp.

The stink of decay washed over Joe, making him gag and almost turn away. "Shit," he coughed out.

"Put some clothes on, grab the car keys, and let's go." The corpse cocked its head, the motion causing ooze to slip down the deep crevices in its neck. "Oh, and better take whatever spare cash your husband has lying around. Think of it as a divorce."

Joe shook his head.

"Uh-huh." The corpse reached over and lifted the receiver on the telephone by the sofa. "What would happen if I dialed 911?" He waved the receiver at Joe tauntingly. "Even if you rush over and stop me from talking, the cops will come to check on the call. Imagine when they find in your boyfriend's apartment a body that's been dead for weeks. At the very least, the romance is over."

"Bitch."

Daley smiled, pulling back all the flesh on his lower face. His teeth gleamed wetly. "Ready to take me someplace warm?"

Thankfully, Daley made it back into the trunk on his own, without Joe having to touch him. Still, he was sure that some residue probably remained in Evan's apartment. His own hands felt the need for scalding water to wash away what he was doing.

The car stalled twice before the ignition caught. He felt like a prisoner returning to his cell. The inside looked and smelled even fouler than he remembered. Gritting his teeth, he put the car in gear and drove away from Evan's building.

At the first gas station he came to open at that late hour, he pulled up to the pump.

"We've stopped." Daley's voice was muffled. Whatever strength he used to move his remains had left him unable to appear as a ghost.

Joe shouted towards the backseat, "We need gas." He took out the tip money he'd stolen from Evan's jeans.

He left the car, paid the tired old attendant behind the thick plastic window, and began pumping.

"That took too long," complained Daley. "It's fucking cold in here."

Joe didn't bother to answer, just stepped on the gas and started driving. He headed for the outskirts of town on the quietest highway. He slowed down as he approached an overpass, stopping on the dark shoulder of the road beneath it.

"What now?"

He got out of the car, bearing the red gas can he had filled at the station. He undid the cap on the plastic nozzle and began splashing the gas over the car, eventually making his way to the trunk.

"Joe? Joe! What the hell—"

"Exactly, Daley." Joe dumped out the rest over the trunk, making sure that the clear stinking liquid splashed into the crevices. He took out the cheap lighter, also bought at the station. "You wanted it warm."

The car began to burn with a sudden whoosh as the gasoline ignited. Joe stumbled back, still hearing the cries from the trunk. As he began to run in the direction he figured led back to Evan's apartment, he felt certain that soon the night would be quiet once more.

AUTHOR'S NOTE

EVENTUALLY, ALL GAY writers tell a hustler story...

While at graduate school, I worked part-time at a gay bookstore in Philly. Nice place but, like many independent booksellers these days, there's a dweomer of sadness about the place, especially at night when it's quiet. At closing, I walked the few blocks to the train station, anticipating my return to suburban New Jersey and my equally quiet and sad apartment.

You know when you're walking along, not so much deep in thought but distracted by something inane that deserves to be forgotten minutes later? Then you see down the block a really handsome guy. So handsome that you come to a halt, as before any captivating piece of art at a museum. He passes and you look into his eyes. Then you turn around in the hopes that he'll glance over his shoulder back at you. Or even—dare you hope?—pause and turn around as well.

I'm an average fellow and never expect my street pirouette matched. But that evening, the handsome young man turned. Surprised by his response, I dawdled before a shop window. A glance saw his approach.

He could have been a gypsy fortune come true: tall, dark, and handsome. I felt slovenly next to his clean-cut, preppy wear. The sneakers alone were a fortune. I guessed him to be in his early twenties. Pretty eyes, full of color, *and the smile he offered flooded my brain with endorphins while adding a dose of adrenaline to my blood.*

I said Hi. He said Hi. We danced awkwardly to the sound of stilted conversation. I noticed he held a little journal, an overpriced Moleskine.

I was in the coffee shop. Just doodling and writing poetry. *He flipped open the book to a sketch of a woman.*

I'm a writer, too.

His smile grew as he asked me what I was doing. I looked past him, in the direction of the train station. Less than a block away. No plans, really. What about you? *I almost stammered the words, apprehensive where they might take me.*

Then he ruined everything. Well, I'm sorta working out here... *He didn't need to say anything else.*

Some of the corners of the "gayborhood" in Philly are manned by hustlers. Depending on how long they've been working the street, blemishes or bruises mar their faces. Their clothes eventually becomes a uniform, ragged, stained and hanging loose around their limbs. As you walk past, they'll whisper an enticement. If you look at them a moment too long, they'll become bold and approach. These are straight boys who'd rather their lips surround a crack pipe than your anatomy.

I felt as if the pavement had been pulled out from under me. No, even worse. I was gobsmacked at finding myself in some parallel world with Hollywood's notion of whores.

I didn't know what to say, how to react, beyond shock.

He asked if I was offended. I told him, You're too pretty. Why would you need to be doing this? At any of these bars, *I said, pointing around me,* guys would be fawning all over you.

Oh, you know how it is. You crave excitement, something forbidden. I wanted to try it out.

I shook my head in disbelief. No, I never thought letting some creepy guy suck me off in an alleyway was fun.

Even the way he shrugged his shoulders was sensual. That's why I'm here with you. You're good-looking and—

I blushed. I become even more tongue-tied when someone compliments me. I wanted to believe him, yet how sincere could a guy offering sex for money really be?

You don't need to be doing this, *I repeated.*

He smiled. When you're gorgeous, you can flash pearly teeth and it becomes dialog.

And I considered his offer. That's being honest. What would have happened had I any money in my wallet? But I was broke, which made things easy.

He shrugged when I told him no but kept the smile and offered, Another time.

During the train ride back to New Jersey, I stared at the landscape rolling past but saw only the boy on the street. I needed to comprehend what had happened. Why would someone not only attractive but charming and clever be hustling? Escorting, fine, that I could understand. He could earn hundreds of dollars within a span of an hour. But boys like him shouldn't be dropping their jeans for a couple of soiled Jacksons.

My dinner had no taste, my bed offered no comfort. I wondered if he had been some sort of lure. I began imagining a gang of homophobic youths waiting down the alley to pounce on whomever he seduced. Or maybe he was a cop, undercover vice?

When I told Rick Bowes what had happened, he scoffed at my rationalizations. Many boys look for excitement that way, he said.

I looked for the young man the next time I worked at the bookstore, but I never saw him again. He remains a mystery and thus, now and then tortures my imagination. My only release is telling his story.

"The secret of life is to appreciate the pleasure of being terribly, terribly deceived."
Oscar Wilde

Time for a true story...

HIDDEN IN CENTRAL ASIA

I ENROLLED IN a graduate class focused on Central Asian culture, with a two-week trip to China and Mongolia. The professors heavily stressed the need for a "buddy system" and so I paired up with D—, a fellow who seemed pleasant but reserved. That was an understatement. In the days before the trip, I watched him take copious notes, fold papers along the proper creases, and measure out the words to every statement. At the airport terminal, he would repack his carry-on bag now and then. Conservative, anal, and rigid, he seemed incompatible with my messy, loud gay life.

Though I seem extroverted, new situations leave me anxious and wanting to hide. So I decided to play it quiet, subdued. To pretend to be straight. I worried that one of the academic chaperones might know the truth; didn't my emails to them have telling signatures, hints of the sort of stories I wrote?

Always on guard, I muffled my speech and gestures, was wary of any details about myself. Though I've never been categorized as flaming, I'm sure the signals that rise off me would register to even bargain-basement gaydars. So I slipped up now and then. But that's getting ahead of myself...

A small number of us took an earlier flight from Philadelphia to Chicago and waited for the rest of the group. On my second sip of a vodka and cranberry juice, the flight attendant walked down the aisle and nudged my arm as she passed. A full glass-worth covered me. A push of the overhead button brought her back. She giggled when I told her what happened and made an odd comment about her tush causing the damage. She brought me bottles of vodka and cans of juice to make amends.

The fourteen-hour flight from Chicago to Beijing was less messy but more fateful. The girl seated next to me admitted to an overactive bladder after she woke me the second time trying to reach the aisle. So I often stretched my legs. At the jet's fore, I saw L—.

Not our first encounter; we'd met months back, while waiting to speak to the class's professor. We had chitchatted about her interest in homeopathic medicine and acupuncture. I once worked for a medical publisher and so knew a little about such things. I had been a scruffy mess from all-night study sessions when she met me then. L—'s beautiful by many standards. Petite and shapely. Blonde hair. Elfin features with a very mischievous smile. I never expected her to remember me.

On the plane, she played cards, nearly falling out of her seat as she laughed. She acted happy to see me and coyly asked me, by name, to bring her another of the tiny bottles of wine they served. I saw a few toppled on her tray and realized that she was drunk. Not tipsy, but roaring drunk. Far be it for me to deny her relief from the boredom of the flight. Ambien helped me sleep through the rest of the flight.

Anxieties over Beijing customs forced the entire class to clump together like sheep through the airport. A sober L— stayed close by me. She made sure that I snapped a single clandestine photograph of the airport's interior; the Chinese authorities must fear international espionage, especially of their billboards for Western brand soda.

L— kept smiling at me during the bus ride. We chatted about how strange it felt to be on the ground, halfway around the world from home. While we went through the routine of showing passports, checking into the hotel, and exchanging dollars for yuan, I gravitated to L—'s friendliness. We seemed like the only people in the group who had any energy after the long flight; the rest of the class left the hotel lobby for their rooms. When L— went outside to enjoy a cigarette, I tagged along.

We sat beneath the gaze of a worn marble foo dog, one of many I'd see over the next two weeks. We laughed and talked while her smoke drifted up to join the pollution hanging over Beijing that warm night. I sat close to her even though the acrid smell bothered me. She wiped sweat from her forehead and wondered if the hotel had a swimming pool; she hoped for a night swim. I mentioned that I hadn't packed any swim trunks. She grinned and told me it didn't matter.

The foo dog should have barked, should have interrupted us at that very moment. What good was a guardian beast if it failed in its role? But the marble dog remained still and I realized then and there that L— had been flirting with me for the past half hour. Worse, I knew that I'd been flirting back.

An admission: as of that summer, I'd been fallow, a dry spell of global-warming proportions. Over four years without a date. No sex for almost two years. I'd forgotten that euphoric feeling when someone attractive grinned at you. When you become aware of each moment of eye contact. When subtle movements of the hand or leg start to sink into your thoughts.

She must have seen my blush; it must have fed her interest.

So caught, I didn't want the attention to end. I wondered when I should attempt to kiss her and whether straight people kiss differently.

We went back inside. The woman behind the courtesy desk informed us the hotel lacked a pool but did offer massages. If L— was disappointed, I never knew because she started talking about all the health benefits a massage offered. Her excitement swept me along. I never gave thought to refusing.

In the lower basement, a great many young women lounged about the massage parlor's dimly lit waiting room. One of the services they offered was a Thai massage for a hundred yuan (little more than fifteen US dollars). My suspicion that sum would buy the fabled "Happy Ending" my straight gaming buddies back home indulged in was proved correct at the end of the trip, when another classmate confided that he'd visited the parlor and one of the masseurs grabbed his dick. The poor guy, so uptight, had panicked and fled before any release.

L— and I chose to the simple, full body massage as a couple. They led us into a small room featuring two padded tables. Our masseurs spoke very little English and gestured for us to strip before lying down.

I'd never had a massage before and thought my briefs had to go. I may have traumatized my masseuse—a woman for me, a man for L— —who became frantic and told me not to drop everything. I was so focused on the masseuse's stage fright that I missed L— undressing. Without my glasses, I couldn't see any fine details, anyway. Wrapped by towels, we lay on our stomachs and let the masseuses go to work.

After five minutes, I wondered why in hell anyone would ever want a massage. That woman pounded and smacked my neck, shoulders, and upper back with such fervor, I came to the conclusion some American tourist had in the past wronged not only her honor but three generations of her family. I would have cried out in pain if the breath wasn't forced out of my lungs with each slap. For days afterward, I winced with each step.

Not L—. She kept up a merry patter of guidebook Mandarin with the masseur. Charmed by her, they brought us complimentary cold drinks to sip during a brief break in the assault and battery.

I glimpsed L—'s small breasts while she dressed, and she accepted my gallant offer of help with the button. I leaned in and kissed her for several minutes. We came close to stripping again.

The Gay Gods would punish me later. But right then, they acted like total bitches and remained quiet as we made out more in the elevator. In the hallway, near our rooms, she straddled my lap. My hands played all over her jeans, foreign territory that I'd never been so eager to explore. She alternated coy with bold, and blamed me for the latter reaction.

I loved telling stories. So I began one about my high school senior trip and another girl in another hallway. Fiction, of course; the most sordid thing I'd done in Disneyworld then was jack off to memories of classmates, cocky and shirtless, as they stood in lines to the waterpark rides.

Eventually we pried ourselves apart. Of course I had trouble falling asleep. Culture shock. Not from being thousands of miles away from home but because of an American girl. I worried that I might be bisexual, and had tricked myself for the past three decades to ignore a gender.

Of all the letters in that GLBTIQ alphabet mix, B's have the worst reputation, reinforced by the wisdom of film festivals: one can't trust bisexuals. Aren't they liable to abandon you for a member of the opposite gender, humiliating you in the process?

But beyond this potentially horrible new label lurked the fact that I self-identified as a gay writer. True, not always with capital P-ride, but for the past few years, nearly everything I'd written had gay characters, sensibilities, and themes. I mentioned coming out on my website. As I tossed back and forth under the stiff covers of a Beijing hotel, as my uptight roommate snored peacefully—no doubt sleeping confident because he'd return from this trip without any secrets to hide from his fiancée!—I wondered what I should do about my gay website, my gay stories, my gay friends...what would they all think?

I'd taken a few undergrad psychology classes and always favored Erickson, with his stages of self-actualization. Sure, I was floundering in the adult limbo of Intimacy vs. Isolation, but I'd been confident in achieving an identity. But that night left me questioning everything. Identity vs. role confusion, that stage when adolescents struggle to reconcile how they appear to others with how they feel inside.

I woke still troubled. I finished my first exposure to authentic Chinese food, an unsatisfactory breakfast in the hotel dining hall. I worried that the snakes, crabs and fish crowded in dingy tanks, near where I found the coffee and faux orange drink, would be served as dinner. L— arrived late and sidled up against me with a smile. Though I'd already eaten, I stayed with her while she nibbled on safer, Western-style selections.

On the tour bus to the first day's sites, Tiananmen Square and the Forbidden City, she sat beside me. We walked together and, while exploring the Palace Museum, now and then we held hands, which thrilled me as much as the ancient architecture and artwork. My experience dating men involved few instances where I'd ever dared held his hand in public. But with a girl... It felt so bold, so grand, and left me giddy with school-boy mischief. I asked L— if she'd ever heard the legend that kissing someone within the walls of Gugong Bowuyuan meant a thousand years of shared happiness. More fiction. Near stonework dating back centuries, we tested my legend.

The following evening a few of us decided to explore part of downtown Beijing and eat with the locals. L— and her roommate accompanied me and mine. The girls wanted to go shopping and D— needed a gift for his fiancée. I tagged along. We found a decent-looking restaurant that had a nice crowd and were brought upstairs (a trend that would often happen whenever we went out to eat in China; I had the distinct feeling that the restaurant staff were hiding Westerners away from the rest of their patrons, as if embarrassed or bothered by our presence or the good manners not to stare at us).

We'd all been warned against drinking the local water. Many places didn't sell bottled, so the alternatives were tepid cans of soda, hot tea, or liquor. L—didn't suffer; the only time during the trip I ever saw L— drink water was while exploring ruins or hiking. Otherwise...well, the girl liked her booze. I drank about as often as I went to a Broadway musical or ate fondue, maybe once a season. And I liked musicals and loved fondue. But all the Berman men were lightweights when it comes to alcohol and a guy very dear to me died drinking and driving, so I was cautious. So cautious that I never recognized the opportunity to have a drink when offered and rarely mourned missing such chances.

Somehow I became the de-facto leader on most of our outings even though my Chinese was limited to mispronounced "Hello" and "Thank you." The menus often had no pictures and limited, if any, English. That night, the girls wanted to order wine with dinner and I chose one randomly. Based on the inexpensive price, I figured the bottles would be small and asked for three. The waitress seemed confused and questioned my order. I repeated myself, several times, even in Chinese with the help of D—'s guidebook. Each time, the waitress became more distraught until she finally called over our heads to the hostess/female maître d'. That woman had a better grasp of English and gestured that the bottle was large. We all laughed.

Our "wine" arrived before the food. The waitress brought me a paper box. I noticed its thick coating of dust. Bad sign number one. She lifted out the heavy bottle, which lacked the graceful tapering shape common to wine. I stared down at a clunky glass jug reserved for hard liquor, the contents clear as water. Bad sign number two. I couldn't read the label, of course, but the United Nations must demand that spirits present their % of alcohol printed on the label somewhere in Arabic digits. Alcohol, the true universal language. An undergrad education from New Orleans had taught me enough to understand that *180* meant the "wine" was 90% alcohol. Now I understood the waitress's distress over my ordering multiple bottles: concern over being blamed for the alcohol poisoning of five Americans.

When I told the others, we shared a mix of astonishment, slight dread, and curiosity. I unscrewed the lid and bad sign number three hit my nose, and 90% evaporated in an instant to clear my sinuses.

Since I'd been the one to pick the drink, I had to go through with having a little. I poured a shot's worth into my glass and took a sip. Can a drink be called smooth if it flows down your throat like molten lava? Should you cough or not? Is tearing permitted? All three happened. I re-christened the concoction "firewater" and the nickname stuck throughout the trip. D— tried a little sip. L— tried more than a little. I finished off my shot. I never remembered how the food tasted.

Our cab driver padded the fare by taking a very long, convoluted path back, but that gave me time to sober up enough to turn down L—'s invite to go out clubbing. I remembered she was twenty-four, but my dislike of nightclubs hadn't much changed from when I was that age. So despite her pleas for me to come along, which approached whining, I said no and returned to the hotel to sleep off the poison I'd drunk.

The next morning, we boarded the Trans-Mongolian Railroad headed for Ulaan-Baatar, the capital of Mongolia. L— and her roommate pulled D— and me into a compartment (each accommodated four passengers on narrow folding bunks) so they wouldn't have to share the cramped space with anyone else. I'm thankful for not being claustrophobic. The Beijing summer had reached ninety-some degrees and the train window wouldn't open all the way to allow much of a breeze. With four 98.6s confined to a small area the compartment became oppressively hot. A tiny, archaic fan near the ceiling only annoyed my peripheral vision.

The girls informed us that the bathrooms were the worst ever: dirty cubbyholes that reeked of urine. I pitied their need to have to sit down to pee; I could stand and aim for the steel bowl, which led directly to the tracks rushing below. We later discovered that the bathroom doors automatically locked whenever the train stopped to discourage stowaways; this didn't seem an issue early in the trip, but, as we would all find out, would become a nightmare for many.

On one top bunk, D— arranged his stockpile of supplies, including several bottles of liquid. The only thing he shared was beef jerky, which made us thirstier. Each car had a near endless supply of water, but it came piping hot from the spigot. We started filling cups and empty bottles, so that by nightfall they might have cooled. The club car had strict hours and limited seats, so often I missed eating because of being too early or late or because some group of hostile Germans invaded our territory.

At the far bottom bunk, L— cuddled against me. Now and then we sneaked a kiss. She often whined about the heat, and I gave her a sleeping pill. Well, it might have been an antibiotic—my father slipped it into my dopp kit. Whatever it was for, she fell asleep for hours. The rest of us meandered back and forth, getting to know the rest of the class better. One professor had brought along his family, including his fourteen-year-old daughter and her best friend, and this pair of geeky and goofy girls entertained us with MadLibs and silly card games.

The entire train ride would be thirty-plus hours (the railroad followed an old trade route from China to Russia). By evening, the train had stopped several times, including for security checks by dour uniformed Chinese officials and soldiers. The heat sapped the energy from all of us, but made sleep difficult. Then, the train came to a halt. After an hour remaining still, we learned that Mongolian tracks were based on Soviet-era design and incompatible with Chinese-manufactured tracks. The entire train had to have its wheels changed before it could continue, a process that takes roughly four hours.

Remember those horrible bathrooms? Well, for the next four hours they were locked shut. The girls whined, bemoaning all the cooling water they had drunk. I wanted sleep, but had gallantly chosen the top bunk and my acrophobia decided that six feet off the ground resembled sixty. Plus, I was convinced the nearby fan blade, which lacked a proper cage, would snip off my fingers during the night.

Once the train started moving again, and the long line of women outside the bathroom doors dispersed (and a collective sigh happened across the entire train), I managed to drift off...only to awaken hours later to a sandstorm invading the compartment. Wind carried the grit from the desert we crossed through the tiny window we'd left open. Everything in our compartment was soon covered in sand and dirt, including all the cups of water, my blanket, our exposed skin. I couldn't close the window and the temperature plummeted to freezing.

A lovely ride. By the time the train arrived in the capital of Mongolia, each of us was frazzled, exhausted, thirsty and hungry. L—'s whining grated on my nerves, especially when she began a litany of "Me hungee." Do straight men enjoy listening to baby talk? I quickly came to despise it, but I kept my mouth shut. Suffering in silence seemed more appropriate to the surrounding Eastern culture, though Genghis Khan would have thrown her off the train the first time she started pouting.

At the hotel, we discovered 1970s style tube showers. Or something from *Logan's Run*. As I threw my luggage on the floor, I hoped L— would knock at the door and join me in depleting Ulaan-Bataar's hot water reserves, rinsing off the accumulation of sweat and dust storm. I thought being physical with her would chase away my earlier annoyance. But she went directly to her room.

No drama happened that night as everyone recovered from the terrible train ride. Maybe because I ate dinner at the professors' table and enjoyed some much-needed intelligent conversation over exotic lamb dishes.

The next day, we toured local pharmaceutical manufacturers (originally the class had been *Ethnopharmacology in Central Asia*, but Rutgers University discovered if they wanted to fund the trip they needed to enroll more than two students so other fields of study were encouraged). I took some photographs of rose-flavored condoms made by one factory. Sadly, testing was not permitted.

L— and her roommate were more interested in shopping. Ulaan-Bataar's streets weren't the safest. The pavement had more craters than the moon due to countless freezes and thaws. Drivers ignored all signs. Wild dogs roamed the streets. Though the capital had plenty of streetlights, there was no money to ever turn them on.

So I came along on the walk to the Mongolian equivalent of a shopping mall on the pretense of protection, but really to serve as a beast of burden. As part of my new straight persona, I relied on every clichéd television episode I'd ever watched: long sighs at having to wait while they tried on tops, resigned shrugs when they asked my taste in color or style, and volunteering to carry every bag. On the walk back to the hotel, L— told me more about her family, especially her wayward brother. She resented how close he was to his best friend and suspected there was more than just a bromance between them. The thought that her brother might be gay and keeping it a secret left her flushed with anger. She told me how much she hated lies. I felt a growing sense of dread.

That night a bunch of us decided to explore the city. Our guide had mentioned that the majority of people in the capital were under thirty, so it seemed lively. We chose a German restaurant—most of the places to eat catered to foreigners—and, as we sat down at the table, L— whispered to me, without provocation, "If you break my heart, I'll cut your balls off."

I blinked in shock and my insides went cold and taut. I didn't say a word to her while ordering or eating the first bites. She rubbed my back. "Baby, what's wrong?" In more of a mutter, I asked her how she expected me to react when she just threatened me with amateur castration. She became all sweet and fooled me. I think I wanted to be fooled.

Later that night, five of us (including L— and her roommate and thankfully two other guys, not D—) went clubbing. I let the girls choose where. There were countless well-dressed young men hired by clubs as barkers. On the sidewalks, they called to passersby, especially tourists.

We followed one handsome guy upstairs. Erotic artwork decorated the stairs and we suspected he was leading us to a strip joint. We were ushered into a private room behind the bar. Tacky gold drapes made the walls shimmer. Faux Grecian statues clashed with late-eighties furnishings. We anticipated dancing girls but only a waiter with Korean beer came in. We waited, sipping the acrid beer, but nothing else happened. We peered through the door and saw the club beyond empty, the music blaring despite the lack of patrons. The bartenders and staff offered nervous smiles. Soon bored, we left. Downstairs, the girls were drawn by the promise of people dancing to thumping music.

The crowd was young, with a penchant for inner-city style and clothing, and clumped together trying to emulate MTV. I led L— out on to the dance floor and the others followed suit.

My internal metronome has remained stuck on Duran Duran for years, so I didn't recognize the beat. I thought all the local guys acted cute with their youthful posturing and trying to be all hippity-hoppity and gangsta. I struggled to pay attention to L— and not my surroundings. When pairs of Mongolian boys started dirty dancing with each other, my neck developed a cramp. I noticed there were a lot of young guys in the club. As my footsteps shuffled, I realized it was nearly all guys. L— and her roommate were treated by the locals as if they were something new.

Then I saw a bunch of guys head for a side door—the bathroom, I assumed. A bunch of "giggling like schoolgirls" guys. I wondered if Mongolian culture embraced the pack-urination mentality, not at all common with guys in the States.

On the dance floor, the locals began brushing up against not only the girls but us boys, intimidating the rest of us. Well, not me. I had spied a young guy leaned down to whisper something in his handsome friend's ear. Only, from my angle it looked like he was sucking on that earlobe.

So then it hit me. This must have been the first dose of my punishment by the Gay Gods. Bitches. I moved closer to L— to tell her we might be in a gay club.

L—'s roomie desperately wanted to leave and began pulling L—'s arms. Regretfully, I agreed and led them back through the darkness.

I couldn't sleep that night. My thoughts were consumed with packs of sweaty and smiling young Mongols, a horde I wanted to rape and pillage me. I couldn't even jerk off because in the next bed was D—, snoring in time with the pariah dogs' howls beneath my window.

As I began devising my plan to return to the club, a rare moment of self-awareness struck me. An emotional epiphany. The whole reason I'd fallen so hard and fast for L— was entirely, and sadly, selfish. Of course, one could argue that every romance begins with purely selfish motivations. But since it had been so long since anyone showed any interest in me, the next encounter with someone I found physically pleasing who flirted with me, wanted to kiss and touch me, and enjoyed my attention...how could I not be smitten?

My need for companionship had overcome gender.

In elementary school, whenever they would dim the lights to show a film, I would try and put my arm around the nearest girl. Teachers called my parents, who discovered I'd been mimicking what I saw on television.

But whatever attraction I had felt for them dimmed by junior high school. When I wasn't daydreaming about boys, I was devising layers of indifference to hide my newfound interests. I had nothing to pattern myself after. My indifference to romance led all my high school friends to think I was asexual.

I hid too well.

I didn't have that first, real kiss until college. Followed by disastrous fumbling, shame, remorse, all the drama one expects from a rushed, desperate first time. Then came too many years of dating mishaps. In my twenties, I made the same mistakes my straight friends had when they were teens. Each mishap wore away at my self-esteem until it seemed better to return to hiding than risk being hurt.

L— made me feel good about myself. Clever, witty. Even after a long-ass train ride, when I couldn't have looked or smelled my best, she never shied away from being physical with me.

But when faced with my preferences, after seeing the very cute young men in the club, I had trouble recalling the passion for L— I had felt only forty-eight hours earlier. Rather than feeling a sense of freedom, I felt awful for abusing her interest in me. Yet I couldn't deny I wanted to go back to the club, felt I belonged there—not for its drinks and music and dancing, but as a member of that tribe.

The next day the class toured more of the city. At night, L— pressed me to go out with her but I said I was too tired. When she went up to her room, I made my move. I had been carrying a pocket flashlight the whole time—remember how dark it gets? Well, Ulaan-Bataar's roads and pavements were rocky traps after countless winters' freezing and spring thaws. I didn't want to fall into a pothole in the dark and get eaten by one of the packs of wild dogs I had seen hunting through the streets.

So I went out by myself—a strict no-no according to the professors. The walk to the club seemed longer than I remembered and my nerves were on edge. I didn't want to be seen and hid when I nearly stumbled onto some fellow students out on their own.

I finally found the club. Deserted.

I'm reminded of those terrible EC Comics stories. The ones where the weird little shop or bazaar vendor sold the hero a monkey's paw or faulty genie lamp and, when he goes back to confront the merchant, the stand has disappeared. It was as if there had never been a Gay Night in Mongolia. I sipped bad Korean beer and waited for the young homos to come giggling in but they never did. I had missed my chance and the Gay Gods laughed and laughed as they observed my agony.

But their final bit of torture awaited my return. For though I'd been so cautious and seemingly clever when I left the hotel, my fallen spirit had left me careless as I returned. I came walking up to the hotel and saw, too late, L— sitting outside smoking a cigarette and chatting with another student. She, of course, saw me. I should have simply said hello and headed up for my room but, guilt stricken, I sat down with them and listened to the conversation as an icy air descended. When she went up, she made a caustic remark about my being so sleepy.

I began to dread the rest of the trip with so many days remaining abroad and alone. I received a cold shoulder for a day. By then everyone else in class knew that something had happened. D— even seemed sympathetic as he handed me a note from L—. Shades of high school, well, of a high school cliché that had never happened before to me. L— thought I was angry with her. She showed up at my door and we chatted outside in the hall and I lied and told her I'd needed some space the other night and so went out for a walk. She accepted the story with ease and I told her I wanted to be friends for the sake of the trip (after all, who else would I room with on the return thirty-hour train ride?).

On the bus to the ger camp, she took the seat in front of me. We chatted for a few minutes and then she told me how uncomfortable leaning over the seat to talk was. She asked if she could sit next to me and I couldn't really refuse. Before I knew it she was cuddling up against me and we were holding hands. I could see why I've never had a boyfriend—I lack judgment skills.

At the ger tent we camped at, I learned many things. The Mongolian countryside is beautiful and has the cleanest air I have ever breathed (my asthmatic lungs sigh, lovesick for it). Also, some of the other girls on the trip, the wealthy daughter of the family vet, the fourteen year olds, had crushes on me. Their mothers were worried they would jump me in the ger. What the hell? I go through an era where no one wants me and suddenly every available girl is hitting on me. When did I lose my gay scent? Why weren't these guys? Okay, not the fourteen year olds, that would be icky, but a vet's son would have been promising. At least I could have earned my kitty some free shots.

Anyway, L— and her roommate wanted to drink, of course, so they bought all the alcohol they could at the ger camp. Well, they balk at the traditional Mongolian aperitif, fermented mare's milk, which I actually tried and enjoyed (tastes like carbonated buttermilk). It wasn't enough and the firewater from Beijing made a return appearance in a drinking game. The scoring methods involved accruing points—bad in this case—for being the oddball and not having done something others had. L—'s sordid past made her the first loser, not that she minded. The virginal, uber-geek math student won. I was tipsy enough while playing that I would have admitted to having anal sex but I had enough sense in me to lie about kissing a boy. Still, we were loud enough—especially when I bragged about having a three way once (well, twice) that my department chair knocked on our door to tell us to quiet down. Guess the Mongolian steppes have censors.

By the time we returned to Beijing, I felt eager to return home and to normalcy. The charade with L— left me tense and on edge. Even the pleasure of fooling around with her (she was a good kisser, I readily admit) faded fast. She asked me if we would be dating back in the States. I lied to her again and again and felt terrible for it.

We never had sex sex. Neither her roommate nor mine had the civility to be scarce long enough. We came close. Twice.

In Ulaan-Bataar, I mentioned to her how all the cuddling and kissing without...release had left me more than a bit uncomfortable. She giggled. When her roomie took a shower, L— swore that she could suck me off in under ten minutes, and thus before her roomie saw us. I had my doubts but dared her to prove it. I'm sorry to say, but her oral talents stopped with kissing. After five minutes of lip and tongue abrasion, I took matters into my own hands. Since it had been two weeks, I didn't last long. But the mess was awful, all over me, the sofa. I had to wipe everything off with my shirt. She was giddy, though, at winning the dare. I never told her I imagined hot Chinese guys pedaling rickshaws during the final minutes.

Then, on our final night in Asia, we were in my hotel room while D— checked his email downstairs in the business suite. Despite my patience worn thin by her antics, I found myself eager to touch her. Soon, most of her clothes came off. My lips roaming her neck, her face, I then whispered to her "I want to fuck you in your a—" I caught myself just before finishing ass, the syllable squirming on my tongue. She must have not caught my near-Freudian lapse. Then, D—'s knock on the door. I guess I should be grateful.

As we traveled to the airport, her ugly, possessive nature became more and more evident. Our tickets had assigned seats, and she whined over being apart during the flight home. I secretly rejoiced. She insisted the fellow who had the assigned seat switch with her. When customs held her back, I told him to sit down and soon confided in him how smothering she was. He admitted he had wanted to get with her at the beginning of the trip but soon realized he was happy she had chosen me. Booby prized as it were.

I pretended to sleep when an irate L— came over during the flight and basically threatened the poor guy if he wouldn't switch with her. She came back again, later, when I was eating. I was caught, and told him he could move. All smug and happy she sat down and spent the rest of the flight insulting my interest in cartoons, asking about what we'd be doing back home, and trying to get frisky.

When we arrived in Philadelphia, her parents met her at baggage. I avoided all of them until she came up and asked for the phone number exchange. I quickly left after giving her my cell.

Whenever I wanted to stop dating someone I played Not-Home, Not-Answering. Yeah, pathetic, but I hated confrontations. So I ignored her calls and text messages. Several calls, every day, and lots of texting. I figured she would get the hint and believe me a total asshole who only wanted a fling.

But then one afternoon a couple weeks later, while heading out the door, I noticed the rose in the mailbox. I would never have thought such a pretty flower could leave me so chilled. I forget if *Fatal Attraction* had an official theme song, but one was playing up and down my spine. How the hell had she uncovered my folks' address? To this day I have no idea. But I had to make a decision, as she could stop by at any time. So I came out to my parents. Not as gay, of course. They'd known that for a decade. No, as having had a hetero-affair. Oh the mocking! My dad started referring to L— as Lady Rose. I would be upstairs and hear him try to sneak to the door, opening it and calling up, "Steve, Lady Rose is here for you!" I now know my sense of humor is genetic.

So I started replying to her texts and emails, telling her to stop calling, that it was over. She would not accept that, becoming by turns belligerent and cajoling, threatening and sweet. Very creepy. I finally emailed her and told her the reason it would never work was because I was gay. I expected that to be the end, but she accused me of lying, that I could never be gay, I was too smooth. That left me dumbfounded. Me smooth? I struggled to convince her, told her about my writing, my website, but she insisted on remaining ignorant.

Finally, I met her in person, at a Borders. We had the scene where she cries and I feel like a worm as I apologize for deceiving her, abusing her. (I stayed silent about any fooling around having been consensual). She told me it didn't matter, that she loved me. She went so far as promising I could still see guys on the side as long as we remained together. Clearly, her grasp on reality had never come home from the Far East. Once I felt certain she knew we wouldn't be buying a house with a white picket fence, I walked away. She tried a few more times to get together but I never responded.

I regret hurting L—. I had traveled to China and Mongolia to explore new cultures but underestimated the hazards: not of foreign lands but being foreign to myself. But realizing you're lonely and hurting yourself by hiding away—whether through deception or remaining in your quiet apartment—becomes a Pyrrhic victory if you find yourself frightened by the very thought of dating again. As I finish these words, I glance at my calendar and realize it has been years since I walked strange new lands and felt the thrill of another's hand in my own, now stranger still.

AUTHOR'S NOTE

I REMEMBER WELL the last time I saw Mike: he'd been dead for a number of years.

I HAD A date one autumn night. With a girl. Long hair and longer legs. I'd become so miserable being gay that I tried again to "straighten out" and date girls again. I don't remember how I met her. Probably she worked whatever boring job I had at the time.

I do remember that she lived in Atco, NJ, off of Burnt Mill Road, which is infamous for its ghost: a boy struck and killed by a truck. This may sound familiar to anyone who might have read my novel Vintage. According to local lore, if you drive down Burnt Mill at a certain hour at night and flash your headlights just so, the ghost appears.

I knew nothing of the story until well after I arrived at her house. This was only my third date ever with a girl and I anticipated we'd watch the videos I brought and maybe kiss. Wasn't that what normally happened for heteros?

Her perfume smelled golden. I fixated on bits of her, one at a time, so as not to dwell on how nervous, how wrong it all felt. Even while stroking her arm, I worried my touch would betray me.

On the couch together, she asked me about my writing. A welcome distraction. After I mentioned selling a couple of horror stories, she moved closer against me and whispered in my ear about the ghost boy on Burnt Mill. She promised to show me the right sequence of lights needed to summon him. I asked her if she'd ever seen a ghost before and she nodded and kissed along my neck. I trembled. I asked her if we could call him that night and she shook her head no.

My ex-boyfriend might be out there. *And the kisses ebbed to punctuation as she told me how late at night he would park his car at the end of her driveway, how he would hide outside her window. He was terribly jealous, she told me. The couch we sat on was right beneath her front window. My hackles rose.*

How jealous? *I asked.*

Smith & Wesson jealous. *She favored me with a grin.* But don't worry, I'll work a spell to keep you safe.

I felt my guts begin to sink. The anxious voice of my conscious told me to Run. Run Now. But I had to ask. Spell? *The only magic I believed in belonged to roleplaying games.*

She nodded and took hold of my hand. I went with her out of reflex; I felt lost, as if I'd stepped off the safe path into uncharted regions. The videos remained on the coffee table. The Invisible Man Returns *and* The Mask of Diijon. *They'd been borrowed from a friend and I should have been more careful. They'd never be returned.*

Her bedroom had plenty of lace and plush pillows. And tall jars with candles. The small broom hanging on the wall could have been bought at any crafts fair. She lifted a pewter chalice from atop her dresser and kissed the pentacle adorning one side. I cast spells. Found a friend a job, kept a snowflake from melting until two a.m., change your license plate so he'll never find you.

Her conviction terrified me.

But I don't do love, *she said. With one swift movement, she tugged the comforter down to our knees.*

Clothes were stripped away. As I touched and tasted her, my breath never stopped whispering to myself a nursery rhyme, the repetition of the Gingerbread Man, as comfort. She laughed. I hope she thought me playful.

But my incantation failed me. When I felt her, my fingers might as well have been gloved. When she touched me, guided me inside her, my nerves refused to pass along any sense of pleasure. My mind might as well have been relegated to a glass of water by her bedside.

Though I tried, I couldn't come. Had I betrayed my body or it me? Or some measure of both? By two a.m., I think we were both exhausted, but I couldn't face the awkwardness of feigning sleep beside her, so I dressed.

She warned me again about her ex. I'll light a special candle for you. *She seemed lost in choosing the right taper and so I let myself out.*

The early hours of October coated my old car with glittering frost. The night was quiet, and too many shadows clustered around the base of the many trees surrounding her house. I felt vulnerable and rushed to get the car door open. I expected the battery to be dead but the ignition roared and, as the wipers began to scrape aside some of the frost, I left her driveway.

A weak stream of dry warm air seeped through the vents, heating mostly the backs of my hands and my nose. The back window remained clouded; the defroster had died long before I'd bought the car. I cursed myself for not trying to clear it off before I drove off but I could not bring myself to pull over on the desolate Burnt Mill Road.

When next I glanced in the rearview mirror, a pair of lights turned the glazed glass milky. Headlights.

Even as I told myself that some other poor guy must have stayed out late that night, thoughts of the psychotic ex-boyfriend filled my imagination. I pressed a little harder on the gas pedal.

The car behind me did not stray from the long, winding road. It crept closer.

I rarely drive over the speed limit, but I found that fear eclipsed any questioning the 25 mph sign I passed. My fingers were bone-white clutching the wheel at 35, at 45, I struggled to watch the road when my eyes only wanted to penetrate the cloudy back window.

At 55, my heart hammered in my chest. The glimpsed houses so forlorn and remote that I believed this stretch of New Jersey abandoned but for me and that other driver. The shoulder of Burnt Mill Road promised so many dark patches, suitable ditches to dump my corpse. That ghost boy would play ball with my head.

And, at 55, new lights flared behind me: the red and blue flashes from an Atco police car. I pulled over to the side of the road. Relief and embarrassment chased fear to the edges of my body: sweat on my forehead and back, a slight tremble to my jaw and fingers.

He asked me if I knew how fast I'd been going. I nodded and then told him why I'd been so afraid. Perhaps I told him too much of that night, but the words rushed uncontrolled.

My story must have evoked some sympathy—or amusement—because he let me go with only a warning.

By the time I reached home, I wanted nothing more than bed. But our dog started to whine to be let outside, so, half-dressed, I stumbled after him out onto the deck so he could take care of business in the backyard. I shivered a bit, but the autumn evening had transformed the many trees into massive dark Pixie Sticks spilling not sugar but leaves all over the ground.

Then I noticed the ghost at the edge of the yard, against the wooden fence that separated our property from the neighbors who kept a pen of rusty barbeque grills. I moved to the edge of the deck, leaned against its railing. Without my glasses, the world's edges had disappeared.

The dog trotted around the yard. So much for animals sensing the supernatural.

Was the afterlife so comical that vague figures beneath pale sheets were the norm? No rattling chains, though. And despite the breeze being clean, no scent of flesh burning, I knew it was Mike.

In the last days of our senior year together, I confided in Mike that I'd slept with a guy. First came screams, then tears. He made me swear never to touch another guy again. I did so to stop his crying, a sight that struck me harder than any of his past slaps or punches. I kept that promise, even after graduation, even after I learned Mike had died. A year, maybe two, passed before I yielded.

I wasn't shocked that he returned to me only after my first night with a girl. I knew him too well. When we were roommates, I learned to anticipate his thoughts, feelings, his needs. The tissue of my body was descended from cells built with the little hairs found in his underwear, the sweat soaked into his pillow, and stolen semen.

Or perhaps the witch had worked magic with her candles.

AND YET, *I can't remember what I told him that night.*

I know I rambled: how grief had brought his divorced parents back together again; of the friends we'd shared at Tulane that now punished me with silence. And on good days, I believe I admitted to his ghost that the girl had been a mistake and that I finally knew who I needed to be.

But on dark days—and there are many of them—I think I only apologized, over and over, as I'd done years ago coming out to him. And I told him how much I missed him, how much I was lonely and lost. Tears made my weak eyesight all the worse.

If only I knew what I told him that night. I think it might reveal where I went wrong, help me from straying tomorrow.

Please, please, please, let me get what I want. I can remember how Mike loved the Smiths, how their break-up saddened him, so why can't I recall this? But the memory skips, like those 45s Mike cherished, to me saying goodbye. As I let the dog inside, did I wipe exhaustion or tears from my eyes?

Now AND THEN I dream of Mike. When I wake, I'm never certain whether to cling to these phantoms (so handsome, so deceptively sweet as to be oddly flirtatious) or to let them fade in the light. If only I knew what I told him that night. Then I'd know if these dreams are a reward or a punishment.

KINDER

ALEXANDER SNIFFED THE damaged book. *The Brim Above the Brow: Meditations on the Chapeau.* His nose caught a blend of must from the foxed pages and an unexpected sweetness. He ran a fingertip along the scalloped edges of the bite mark. Strong jaws but the teeth had to be small. Perhaps a rat? The thought disgusted him. He peered at the bookcase and moved aside the 1902 edition of *Lexicon of European Millinery* and *The Proper Tip: Social Demands of the Bowler*. No droppings, no debris, only the usual dust that Ms. Penn attacked once a week.

He crouched down on his knees. The titles on the lowest shelf were novels and collections. Early editions rendered near worthless by cracked spines and loose pages. Every so often, a Trustee would present a plan to sell one. Had the rats disliked Hawthorne? He pulled out his notepad and scribbled a reminder to ask Mr. Cassey to bring his poisons early this season.

For the next few hours, Alexander searched the rest of the study for any other damage or misplaced objects. He found the remains of a lollipop underneath Grueller's mahogany desk. Wine-colored sugar crystals clung to the worn Persian rug.

"Children," Alexander muttered to the empty room.

He wore gardening gloves while removing the offending stick. Alexander had heard somewhere that a dog's mouth was cleaner than a child's. He imagined both as drooling pits.

He had asked the Board on several occasions during his years as caretaker that Grueller House not admit any person under ten years of age, no matter how many adults were present. How could a child appreciate the historical worth of Pennsylvania's—arguably the entire Eastern seaboard's—preeminent late-nineteenth-century hatter? Bored tourists who stumbled upon the sidewalk sign were bad enough. Alexander shuddered whenever someone other than the quiet graduate students or powdered old women from the Historical Society came through the front door.

After one last walk through the house, Alexander turned off the lights and headed upstairs, his feet avoiding the bald patches on the runner. He went through the second-floor hall, with its thirteen coat racks capped with russet derbies, tan fedoras, and homburgs of dusty silver felt. Past the master bedroom, Grueller's changing area had been refurbished for the caretaker's stay. Crème-colored walls held the early summer's heat, and Alexander stripped down entirely before slipping into bed. He closed his eyes and listened to the house groan.

=

STANDING BEFORE THE hallway mirror, Alexander adjusted the hat, which resembled a pale thimble ornamented with a white satin band and silver buckle. He hid the price tag. The gift shop offered replicas of Grueller designs. Boxes from China filled the basement.

He checked his watch: just shy of ten a.m. and he still had several chores and piles of paperwork unattended. When Henry had been docent, there had been time for everything.

Alexander unlocked the front door.

In the late afternoon, the first visitor arrived: an elderly woman in a bold floral dress smelling of rose water. She tilted her head back and forth while looking around the foyer. "Did anyone die here? Someone important. I'm a mystery writer, you know." She took a gilded pen and small memo pad from her canvas bag. "I'm doing research. I just adore cozies."

"The only cozies used at Grueller House are found in the dining room."

The woman nodded and began scribbling. Her bag toppled the stack of slick brochures on the demilune table.

When Alexander bent down to recover the brochures, the children stampeded past him. An arm smacked the side of his face, and fingers scratched his cheek. Wincing, he checked his face in the mirror. His reflection scowled as he touched the edges of the red marks underneath one eye.

"You should keep those children on a leash." He did not see where they went but heard them running through the house's first floor.

"They aren't my children." She finished whatever notes she'd been making and headed off, not in the direction of the dining room, clearly marked, but the parlor.

Alexander tracked the sounds of gaiety and stomping feet to the front room. A boy in lederhosen and a girl in a blouse and Bavarian skirt ran around a table set with Grueller's tools. They must have come straight from some school play. The Heidi reached for the pair of calipers used to measure the skull, not touched since a tipsy Henry had used them as ice tongs.

"Stop that." Alexander clapped his hands to get their attention. "This is not a playroom. Where are your parents?" He hated how shrill his voice became around children.

The pair stopped on the other side of the table. Spittle filled the edges of the boy's toothy smile and dribbled down to his dimpled chin. The little Heimlich fell to all fours and bit at the nineteenth-century mahogany. Wood crunched and splinters clung to his lips.

Alexander shouted in astonishment and kicked at the kid. The boy's belly felt oddly solid, enough to hurt his toes. The Heimlich rolled and struck a chair. A plump hand reached up to the chair's seat.

"That's priceless. Off, off!" Although Alexander knew the chair wasn't an authentic Chippendale but a weak reproduction limited by the unimaginative splat.

The Heimlich nodded and started gnawing at a leg. Heidi came over with a mouthful of feathers. She clutched a deflated down pillow.

"Get out! Out, out, now." He grabbed them by their ears and pulled them towards the door. They snarled in some Alpine tongue. "No unattended children at Grueller House." He hoped they did not belong to one of the Trustees, the majority of whom were lawyers.

The pair stared at him from the sidewalk a moment. Then the Heidi bent down to nibble on the step's wrought-iron railing. Heimlich scratched his pudgy head and yawned, showing a mouthful of endless teeth leading to a very red gullet.

He slammed the door shut and turned the deadbolt. He leaned against the wood while he caught his breath. He'd call for Mr. Cassey and demand he spray tomorrow. Then he'd have to speak to someone at Winterthur about restoration. And the Trustees would have to be involved.

Scrolling through the long list of contacts on his cell phone, Alexander paused at Henry's name.

They had not spoken in the weeks since the Trustees had dismissed Henry. If not for a forthcoming article on Grueller in the *Journal of the History of Ideas*, Alexander might have also been let go. The gratitude at being given a second chance turned to shame whenever he thought of calling Henry.

At night, Alexander found he couldn't ignore the house. The walls felt brittle, the rooms no longer had a sense of refinement and seclusion but left him anxious. He missed Henry's soft voice, the way his snores sounded more like repeated sighs.

In the kitchen he was horrified to find the large woman who wanted cozies with her head in the Oberlin stove, one of the few surviving in Pennsylvania. Murmurs of regret over failing to bring a tape measure echoed in the oven. Her dress had caught on the oven's lower ledge to expose a glossy lavender-shaded slip and legs covered with ruddy blotches.

"Madam," Alexander said with a gasp. He imagined a swift kick to her posterior but that might wedge her tight. "Remove yourself from the Oberlin." He was relieved that cast iron resisted scratching.

She scuttled back and blinked at him for a moment. "Just as well.

They're all convection these days." She made further notations before rising to her feet.

After escorting her back to the foyer, he unlocked the door for her. He took notice that she paused by the bronze box for donations bolted to one wall. She even lifted the swinging lid and peered inside.

He took a firm hold of her arm and guided her to the door. "We have no mysteries here."

=

CARETAKERS WERE NOT permitted to cook their meals on the Oberlin. Not that Alexander had known the urge to chop wood. In the back utility room, he heated a can of Krimmel's Old Pepper Pot Stew over a portable electric burner. He stabbed apart a congealed lump, suspected of being tripe.

Around him, Grueller House groaned. Alexander paused in his stirring and listened. Strong winds would turn the plaster walls into a bellows. He wondered if the house found comfort in creaking. Then he heard laughter.

He went into the hallway. Most of the house was dark. Something short dashed from one room to the next. Giggles and grunts trailed behind it. Floorboards creaked beneath Alexander's argyles.

He could hear the sound of their chewing, a cacophony of rippling cloth, breaking wood, and cracking glass. Their lips smacked. Mastication. Gulps as they swallowed.

He turned on the parlor's lights. Heimlich and Heidi looked up from where they sat on the floor, the remnants of the furniture on their wet cheeks and chins. Their wide eyes had tiny blue dots in the center.

The pair retreated behind the curtain, their fat bellies bulging the muslin. Thick fingers clutched the fabric's edge. Four shiny patent-leather shoes gleamed at the bottom.

"I'm calling the cops," Alexander said as he walked over to them. "They'll take you to dank cells where rough men pee in corners!"

He pulled aside the curtains and found the shoes were empty. Without arms, without hands, the fingers toppled to the floor like Weisswurst, sickly pale and wrinkled at the knuckles.

Alexander didn't call the police. His hands shook as he opened the bottle of Wasmund's Single Malt, he'd bought days ago as an apology to Henry. The first sip of whiskey went straight to his sinuses. He only realized he'd left the burner on when he wandered to the back of the house and smelled burnt stew and pot, an acrid combination. He finished off the single malt as his dinner.

=

MR. CASSEY ARRIVED the next day as Alexander catalogued the damage. The exterminator's navy uniform had a patch on the front (*Francis*) and a silhouette of people standing around an immense, upturned beetle on the backside. Mr. Cassey smelled like cigarette smoke; he had once told Alexander that only the two packs a day habit protected his lungs from the toxins he used.

"So, any more rat sightings? They're a colony. Not a swarm."

"No, I think it's German children." Alexander suspected that the house's insurance policy might not cover such damage.

"Oh, then it's a hamelin of Kinder. Very dangerous. Are they Weimar or Nazi?"

"They're German, isn't that bad enough?" Alexander blinked. For a moment, Mr. Cassey's name patch had read *Franz*. "Um, they might be Alpine."

Mr. Cassey nodded. Then he tore the cellophane off a new pack, shoving the crackling wad into a pocket. He went back into his van and came out with a lit cigarette and a metal canister.

Alexander took several steps back. He didn't know how flammable Mr. Cassey might be. "Why are these Kinder here?"

A puff of blue-gray smoke emerged from Mr. Cassey's mouth as he scratched an armpit. "Normally happens in winter. They're drawn by the smell of lonely folk."

With the aid of his handkerchief, Alexander waved aside the smoke. "I'm not lonely."

"Witches. Bitches. Bachelors." Mr. Cassey smirked, which bent the cigarette. "Especially lifelong bachelors."

Alexander felt his face flush. "My mother endeavored for years to convey the lofty wisdom she gleaned from her subscription to *Redbook*, Mr. Cassey. She failed to straighten me out," he said while stiffening his back.

Mr. Cassey dropped the cigarette on the street and slipped on an old World War II-era gas mask. The round lenses reflected the world askew; Alexander could not see the face beneath the dark rubber. He had a strange feeling that Mr. Cassey was choosing to reveal his true, insectile face. His voice buzzed. Whatever he said to Alexander while entering the house was incomprehensible.

Alexander remained on the sidewalk. It drizzled slightly, possibly ruining the fez he wore. He wished he had a paperback or sudoku or something to waste the time. He considered heading over to browse the shop windows on Antiques Row.

When the front door opened again, wisps of vapor announced Mr. Cassey's exit. He doffed the mask. "That should take care of them. I also sprayed for enfants."

Once inside, Alexander found several Kinder lying on their backs with limbs close and crooked to their torsos. Each golden-haired Heimlich and Heidi looked exactly alike, down to their rosy cheeks, fading to gray, and swollen tongues poking through dark lips.

It took Alexander a long time to bag all the children. He filled both trashcans and afterwards had legs poking out beneath he lids. He was sure the garbage men would give him grief over taking them.

"Being single is not a crime," he muttered as he dialed Henry's number.

==

ALEXANDER THANKED HENRY for holding the bag of takeout so he could find his keys. Worry made him turn the front door knob too hard. Would he find the foyer a disaster? Gnawed ribs of the staircase banisters, wallpaper peeled like the skin of some fruit, and Teutonic tittering in the air?

He sighed and patted his chest in relief when greeted by welcome tidiness. He walked over to the nearest hat rack and lifted off a Stetson. "Your fav—"

"I think I'll stick with this," Henry said and nudged the brim of a garish crimson and white baseball cap.

"Oh." Alexander attempted a smile.

Henry shook his head. "I suppose knowing the Phillies are one of the oldest baseball teams won't help." He lifted off the cap. The sparse hair beneath was matted.

"It's fine." Alexander patted Henry's beefy forearm. "Let's eat."

He had made sure to spread a tablecloth over the small card table. He took out from the bag a wedge of Saga Blue. The woman at the cheese shop had promised it was Danish, thus safer than Cambozola, but Alexander eyed its mottling warily.

He asked Henry to get a long knife from a drawer to cut the bread, then looked around to see Henry was gone. A staccato of clinks came from the old house.

Alexander rushed to the dining room. He expected Kinder, not Henry removing china from the breakfront. "We shouldn't," he said.

"Don't say these were Grueller's." Henry tipped the plate he held against his chest. The gilded rim was worn in spots. "A Trustee's wife donated the set when she redecorated her Rittenhouse Square apartment."

"I know." Alexander sighed.

Henry set the plate down on the long table. "Did we ever get caught? When we came back from *Giselle*—"

"Your first ballet." Alexander had begged one of the Trustees to secure him excellent seats.

"My first."

"And the first time I ever lit the fireplace." Alexander closed the breakfront.

"After two bottles of wine." Henry laughed. He touched Alexander's cheek with his thick hand. The callus on his thumb scratched at the tapered ends of Alexander's mustache. "Nothing happened. Not to the andirons, not to the screen."

"The chinoiserie screen," Alexander whispered. It had such a lovely image of white pebbles spaced along a lonely path leading to a sweet cottage. His eyes closed as he leaned into Henry's palm. He was aware of the slouch of his own spine, the feel of blood carrying the warmth of that touch throughout his cheek, then face, before descending his neck to spread throughout torso and limbs. How could such a simple gesture weaken him so? "But the Trustees..."

"Tell them you want me here."

Alexander welcomed the onset of apprehension. "This is about your job?" He stepped back from Henry.

"No. I just thought...if I was docent again..." Henry brought up a finger to his mouth and worried the nail with his teeth.

"And the Trustees' disapproval of our...liaisons?" Alexander drew out the last word, turning each syllable to lead.

Henry shook his head. "The Trustees must pay extra for self-hating fags." He headed for the door.

=

THE FIXTURES WORKED in Grueller's bathroom. Wearing the Stetson, Alexander treated himself to a bubble bath in the old claw-foot tub, so massive it took nearly a half hour to fill. The scent of lavender and chamomile did not relieve the knots in his back or the hint of a migraine. The Godiva truffles he'd bought for dessert that night helped a little.

If only he understood the mystery of men as well as he did antiques. He shouldn't be lonely or ashamed of an affair with fellow staff. It was all such a nuisance compared to the task of having an entire house to worry over.

The doorknob rattled. A piece of chocolate dropped from Alexander's hand into the suds with a deep plop. The Stetson followed.

Sweet voices came from the other side of the door as fingers scratched the wood.

> "Hier stehen die Männer vorm Spiegel stramm
> Und schminken sich selig die Haut.
> Hier hat man als Frau keinen Bräutigam.
> Hier hat jede Frau eine Braut."

Alexander heard chewing.

"Go away. I have a gun," he said, clutching the wet Stetson over his groin as he stood up in the tub.

The first Kinder, a Heidi, broke through the thin wood. Half-forced her way into the bathroom. One pigtail with a pink ribbon tied at the end dangled to the tiled floor. She gnashed the fragments left in her jaws. He felt her hungry stare.

"Good Kinder." He held up the box of gold-wrapped chocolates. "Candy?"

The Heidi's round nose twitched. A stream of clear saliva dripped down her mouth.

"Delicious candy." Alexander slowly stepped out of the tub as the Heidi crawled through the hole in the door. A grinning Heimlich peered through after her.

Alexander threw a truffle at the Heidi's feet. She picked up the chocolate and smashed it against her lips, devouring the wrapper as well.

He let the hat fall and crushed it stepping back. He tossed another piece near the tub. The Heidi waddled over. The Heimlich had already begun eating the porcelain sink when he heard the Heidi grunting a sound that Alexander took for pleasure. The Heimlich fought to reach the next piece in time.

Plop! Alexander threw a chocolate into the full tub. Then the rest of the box. The Kinder groped and fumbled up the slick slides before falling into the hot bath. They didn't seem to think about breathing as they dived for the sunken treats.

He pulled on his bathrobe. Two fat bodies began floating face down. The Heidi still clutched a melted truffle in one fist, and the chocolate leaked through the tight grip.

=

HANGING THE TIN *Closed for Renovations* sign before noon the next day on the front door pained Alexander. Sundays brought the most visitors. But he could not permit even one patron to see him taking a hammer to one of the imitation Chippendale chairs, the one gnawed by Kinder. Several times as he swung, the Stetson almost fell from his head.

Whenever his mother would end a whine with "Desperate times calling for desperate measures," Alexander would wince. Now, he found himself muttering the same as he struck that dreadful splat. It splintered with satisfaction.

Sacrifices, not measures, he told himself as he carried the kindling into the kitchen. One proved love through sacrifices. He had left Henry a message, begging him to come to the house for lunch. He had even admitted he'd be cooking for Henry on the Oberlin. After he'd hung up, he regretted leaving a recording of his crime.

Men must demand more than an understanding of historical significance. He fretted over so quickly abandoning his firm beliefs that any single individual paled in comparison to the worth of a hat on a rack or a rare cast-iron stove. He felt cooking this meal to be a bit of sedition, an impious act.

The Oberlin's hinges moaned when he opened the oven door. Alexander felt it appropriate to murmur gentle words to coax the oven back to life. "Such craftsmanship" and "Cold pans, warm hearth."

Deep in the back was the reservoir for wood. The gullet had been empty for decades. He hoped the chimney worked and the smoke would rise.

In the back room, he took from the small refrigerator the makings for lunch. Alexander glanced at the cuckoo clock he'd moved from the kitchen after the first signs of Kinder infestation. He kept meaning to check the old records to see if Grueller really did own a Bahnhäusle from the Black Forest. Now he was more troubled that Henry was late by more than a half hour. He checked his cell phone, then the house phone, for messages but there were none.

The kitchen grew warm as the wood burned.

He conceded that Henry would not come. Perhaps Henry despised him now. He expected a rush of sadness but could only summon up a mild measure of disappointment that threatened to become annoyance. He reasoned, as he laid the veal cutlets on a skillet, that Henry had only earned his heartache after being a constant at the Grueller House. When he had arrived wearing that...cap, he had been almost a different person.

As he lifted one lid from the stove with tongs, the oven trembled like a hound shedding water. That and a clattering sound from behind him made Alexander jump, dropping the skillet and lid with an even louder crash.

Flushed, he turned around. A Heimlich brought one glossy, patent leather shoe down hard on what remained of the tin sign—*for Ren*. He smacked his lips and advanced. Behind it, Heidis dashed from room to room.

With his back against the Oberlin—and he felt the heat through his trousers—Alexander stabbed with the tongs. The Heimlich caught the curved ends in his pudgy fingers and wrenched the tool from his hands. The Kinder began teething on the tongs. The Stetson dropped back and landed on the stovetop. The reek of charred felt filled the small kitchen.

"No," Alexander shouted. "I'm not lonely."

Something shoved him aside and he looked up from the floorboards to see the Oberlin stepping forward on its iron feet. The stump of chimney pipe had broken loose at an angle reminiscent of a shark's fin. Its door and drawers slammed open and closed like so many jaws with flickering tongues of fire.

The slightly burnt Stetson rolled off to land back on Alexander's scalp. The pan of veal landed at his feet.

The Heimlich tried to run but the Oberlin scooped the Kinder inside it. Cries of German lasted only a moment. A new smell, sweet and rich like baked marzipan, chased away the stink of singed felt. Despite his shock, Alexander found saliva filling his mouth.

The Oberlin kept shuffling, leaving the kitchen and entering the hallway. Alexander soon heard more Teutonic cries.

=

ALEXANDER BEGAN RETIRING to Grueller's bed at night. An indulgence. He'd rise early and make sure to change the bedding with fresh sheets and lay the quilt just right. Then, before opening, he'd let the Oberlin roam the house, on guard for Kinder, before leading it back to the kitchen.

Enough lamp oil remained for him to proof his letter to the Trustees asking for an increase to the funds allocated to maintenance. He also adjusted his wording for the new docent ad he'd post tomorrow.

He leaned over the side of the high bed and patted the slumbering Oberlin's chimney stump. It wheezed from every crevice and the house echoed the sound, which Alexander decided must be contentment. Then he lifted off the cotton nightcap warming over the tea kettle atop the stove and went to sleep.

AUTHOR'S NOTE

WHEN I WAS an undergrad at Tulane, I lived in an off-campus apartment, narrow and long. I remember how the air-conditioning units would wheeze through the first few rooms. The deeper one went, the more stifling the air became until it felt that the heat had teeth.

My roommate was the worst sort of bully: he'd laugh while abusing me and his shy dog, while being terrified of hurricanes. By senior year, all the apartment windows had masking tape crossing each pane. The sun and heat baked the tape to the glass and only razor blades scraping slow and steady would remove the Xs. He worried, as well, that the gas line leading to the old oven might rupture and suffocate us in our sleep. During one hurricane alert, I cut my hand on the old, rusty gas valve and had to be taken to the emergency room for stitches and a tetanus shot. How I hated that oven.

I returned to New Orleans one spring for Saints and Sinners, a queer literary conference. After lectures and readings, I'd wander the French Quarter alone, hoping more to discover my lost youth than reacquaint myself with memories. One night, as I walked down a nearly deserted Royal Street, a boy stepped out of a doorway and asked me, Would you pay to hear a poem?

Even if I hadn't found him attractive, such odd busking would have stopped me. I asked how much. He grinned and told me the fee was whatever I felt he was worth.

I'll call him Scott.

This Scott's hair was an untidy mop, and sweat left lines on his bare arms like heroin tracks. He rushed his words, an offer to recite either one of the Masters (he rattled off names but the only one I heard was Poe) or an epic of his own design. Nervous energy seeped from the frayed collar of his T-shirt and the torn knees of dirty blue jeans. Traces of grime at his hairline and neck captivated me. I chose one of his compositions.

Free verse tumbled from his mouth. I felt less lonely hearing him, though I didn't listen to the words. Instead I stared at the dance of his jaw, how he swayed his shoulders when he spoke. Afterwards, I handed him five dollars. If he'd asked for more, if his hand had lingered on mine as I pressed the money into his palm, I would have emptied my wallet. But he acted grateful for the meager amount. He went to the corner grocery store, and through the window I watched him choose a chilled container of sushi.

I never told any of the other conference attendees about Scott. The next night, I walked down the same block. He stepped out as before, repeating his offer, as if he had no memory of me. I suspected he might be some pretty clockwork mechanism that reset in the morning. Then a bead of sweat trailing down the side of his face proved him human. I wanted to catch the drop before it reached the ground.

I took out my wallet when I asked for another poem. And wouldn't a hotel room be more comfortable, I said, the air-conditioning a relief from the stifling heat? He took the twenty dollar bills I offered. He muttered verse as we walked together back to the seedy hotel I had booked for the conference.

Perhaps the Olivier House once offered Old World charm but all I saw was a husk, dilapidated, infested. The furnishings looked more salvaged than antique. One had to navigate a convoluted path, complete with bowing and scraping underneath the abandoned spiral stairwell, to reach a claustrophobic elevator. A staccato clanging along with a generous reek came from the nearby ancient kitchen.

I wondered if its oven could be hungrier than me.

The elevator buttons were bulky knots on the wall. I pushed the topmost, the fourth floor. Though the doors closed, still I heard the brutal sound of the oven door chomping. Scott leaned against the wall and closed his eyes as the car stumbled and rose with a groan. I considered kissing his lips, parted while in breath. When I took a step closer, he lifted a hand, placed it on my chest. But the fingers curled around my damp polo shirt, rather than pushing me away. His fingernails were dirty, the thumb blackened from some injury.

He followed me down the hall to my room. Olivier believed in real keys, not slivers of magnetized plastic. I opened the door. A wave of air chilled the sweat on our bodies.

The bed remained unmade.

[I never saw any maids working at the Olivier. My first morning there, I'd discovered red blotches circling my ankles. The mark of bedbugs. Same had happened to me while traveling through China. When I was done with Scott, I would ask the front desk for a new mattress. They would bring me one I thought was clean but it too was contaminated. I had traded up and found myself with lice.]

How could Scott be deaf to the oven that griped below us? I could hear it above the rasp of the air conditioner. Scott trembled as I slipped my fingers under his shirt and stripped his torso bare. His chest was streaked with dirt and ©1992 tattooed over his heart. I touched the inked skin, then slid down to brush the nipple, sharp-edged from the chill.

I thought he might speak then. Recite another poem. He stayed quiet.

I pushed him down on to the bed. He collapsed like a marionette and lay staring at me. Goosebumps pebbled his skin. I wondered how many days he'd been wearing those boxers.

He was so beautiful. My mouth watered.

But the oven wouldn't rest. I glanced at the door, certain it had torn itself loose and had followed us upstairs. It didn't care that I hadn't tasted another guy in years.

I slid one hand up his neck to his chin, then covered his mouth with my palm. The only warmth in the room may have been the ragged breath that passed his lips and escaped my fingers.

Shhhh, I whispered. But he might not have heard or even cared.

My other hand found the edge of the pale sheet beneath him and pulled it over his body. I held him down as I tucked the sheet around him. I made sure to stare into his eyes as I wrapped him tight, until finally I had no choice but to cover his face.

I lifted him from the bed, cradling him in my arms like a swaddled babe, then struggled to open the door while pressing him tight against my chest. I did not want to relinquish him to another.

Outside, I found only the oppressive heat and the oven's raucous summon. As I carried Scott to the elevator, the bundle became lighter, smaller, less of a burden, until he fit within the crook of my arm as we reached the ground floor.

The rhythm of the oven door against cracked linoleum echoed through me as I walked into the cramped kitchen. Sweat ran down my skin to drizzle onto the twisted sheets that wrapped Scott.

I found the oven squatting in one corner. An ugly beast with a scratched and pitted hide and blackened burners. I grabbed the handle, thick and hot as a bull's nose ring, and opened the oven door. The metal rack tongue hadn't been cleaned in years and the smell... had Mike smelled as charred when he crashed that car and burned alive? My eyes watered from the oven's breath.

I thrust Scott inside, turned the dials and heard the welcome ignition of gas. I would have pleaded with the oven to leave me some morsel, but I knew what a glutton it was.

A TROLL ON A
MOUNTAIN WITH A GIRL

RESOLUTE, OWEN CASHED out his 401K—at a penalty—and set out on his world-spanning tour to be eaten by a monster. He packed two brand-new suitcases: one with comfortable clothes, the other with library books. His plan was to study the books en route and, at each destination, whether English countryside or Nerluc in Provence, to unpack a shirt, pair of slacks, and clean white boxers, and meet his fate looking fresh and neat.

But by the time he had reached F in his notebook—*Fachen-Orkney Islands*—undevoured, Owen had had to make some adjustments, such as washing clothes in hotel sinks with tiny bottles of complimentary shampoo. He could not bring himself to meet death appearing too disheveled.

He went from Europe to Africa, then back to New Jersey—he knew the rational thing would have been to search the Pine Barrens first, being they were an hour away when he began his tour, but the thought of breaking alphabetical order paralyzed him. Finding nothing lurking or skulking anywhere, he grew concerned.

Even Tokyo was turning out to be a disappointment. The English-language guide books were rapturous about cherry blossoms and neon. None mentioned an ancient hag's lair on *Nabekura-yama*. The small town of Tōnō was no better; no one knew her story. Didn't local monsters deserve some press? Even Leicestershire's tour books mentioned the threat of the Black Annis. Not that Owen had lucked upon her.

Waiting for breakfast, Owen paged through the yellowed book of folklore, the sole surviving text he had brought from New Jersey. The rest of Owen's books had been abandoned in hotel rooms around the globe. He sometimes wondered if any of the maids had an interest in the echidna or the tarasque.

Owen always treated himself to a large breakfast before setting out for the hoped-for monster's lair. Back when he worked as an accountant, he had allowed his workplace frugality to bleed over to his home life. Mornings were two cups of instant coffee with artificial sweetener and a piece of rye toast. Originally, he'd thought it an exercise in clever discipline to have a sandwich for lunch that began with the day's letter: Monday was a melt sandwich, tuna, which he could have chosen for the next day but that was always toasted cheese (it was unfortunate that no weekday began with G or C). Wednesday was a wrapped leftover in pita; Thursday more toasted; and Friday he was free to lunch out as long as he did not spend more than 7.00 pre-tax and -tip.

But now, Owen saw no reason not to spoil himself. Every meal might be his last. So he indulged in local dishes, ate things like beans and black pudding or *prima colazione*.

The Tōnō hotel's restaurant was quiet, the waitresses busying themselves folding napkins. Owen sat waiting for plates of grilled fish, rolled omelet, and pickles, with rice, of course. He sipped hot tea, unsweetened; he did not know how to ask for sugar in Japanese and there was none on the table.

"Excuse me, but are you American?"

Owen looked up. The man standing by his table's empty chair looked to be in his late twenties but a good shave and haircut might have lost him a few years. He wore an open, wrinkled button-down shirt, the pale t-shirt beneath even more creased. The knees of his jeans were threadbare.

Owen nodded. "Though some would say New Jersey doesn't deserve to be a state." The joke was more for his own benefit. He was uncomfortable with the unexpected.

The guy smiled and unslung an immense backpack he had been carrying. "Great. Would you mind if I joined you? I've missed English."

Owen sat up straighter and lifted a hand towards the empty seat. "I'm Saul."

"Vacationing student?"

Saul laughed. Owen noticed very large teeth, the bottom set chipped and askew. "Half right. I'll be a teacher, or will be next week in Moriokashi. Thought I'd do a bit of roughing it before I start."

A silent waitress brought over Owen's food and took Saul's order with a nod.

"Have you been to Mt. Nabekura yet?" Owen hesitated to take his chopsticks to the meal. Which to eat first? He couldn't discern what sort of fish it was, so that left it to F. Omelettes should be eaten next, but they were mostly eggs, so that took precedence. But then, pickles were really cucumbers...

"I may go tomorrow. I just want a couple nights indoors on a soft bed."

During the past month, Owen had kept his quest secret. But now, almost at the end, he needed to tell someone, if only to reinforce his hope that today would be his last. So he leaned forward and whispered, "I've been hunting monsters."

=

OWEN WAS REASONABLE. He blamed his mother for only half his fascination with men and monsters. As a child, he spent every weekend with her on the plastic-sleeved sofa in the den. They would each take handfuls of salty popcorn from a big metallic mixing bowl and watch whatever old horror movie was on the UHF station. His father had spent every weekend at the shore, working on his boat, no matter what the season. By the time Owen was old enough to cook the popcorn on the stove by himself, he realized why men named their boats fancy lady names.

They shared a game while they watched. Now and then, his mother would cup her hands over his eyes to block the view of the television set. Never at the scariest moment, usually while something dull was happening. She would gasp loudly, as if the most horrible thing had happened, though, and Owen would laugh.

He stayed up late on weekends because as soon as he went to bed she would start crying. And as he grew older, he began to wonder if his mother hated men. He never mentioned how handsome he thought Colin Clive was, or his troubling daydreams sparked by a sweaty Oliver Reed in *Curse of the Werewolf*. He watched how she half-smiled when the monsters caught the pretty girls.

As an adult, it seemed easier simply not to even attempt dating. He told himself it would only end in disaster. He didn't know the rules of the game, what even to say. He watched one of his co-workers sit on the edge of the receptionist's desk and felt more bewilderment than envy. He avoided all offers to get a drink after work and never attended the annual holiday party.

Spreadsheets gave the day structure. Being an accountant, a proper upstanding one, meant no cheating, no lies. Dinners with his mother helped with the nights, fending off loneliness. At first, after he'd earned his CPA and moved into a nearby efficiency apartment, Owen walked home every Monday and Friday night. Then, after his parents' divorce became final, he added Wednesdays. She never understood how to work the VCR he bought her. When she began forgetting things, such as paying bills or leaving on the oven, he did not hesitate to move back in with her. His old room felt small, but he wore it more like armor than a straightjacket.

Her last year, before the pneumonia took her, was spent at a nursing home. He came over every night after work to eat dinner with her. No sofa, just a mattress surrounded by stainless-steel safety bars. Like a crib for an adult. Her skin had faded to parchment and her fingers were all knuckles clenched around a cotton blanket.

"I want to go home," she would say. But the childhood home she wanted was a small house bulldozed decades ago in upstate New York. He would help feed her while the videotape played Bela Lugosi. "The Count," she murmured around a spoonful of soup that lacked any odor.

"I never drink..." he'd say. His mother answered "Wine," with more strength than she mustered for anything else. He'd kiss her cheek. "I'm gay, Mom," he'd say next. Or "I'm like a three-dollar bill" or once "I could marry in Massachusetts now." It should have been a relief to tell her, but she never reacted, never seemed to remember, and so it was simply one more standard action of his nightly visits like kissing the top of her head, which seemed to have a cradle cap where the hair thinned.

After the funeral, the house seemed far too still. He read about something called Gay Bingo. He knew the rules to bingo. But he never made it to the bar hosting the event. Along the way, he passed a pair of young men walking hand in hand. They reminded him of the boys in contemporary horror films, always more gorgeous than the damsels in distress. They looked like dolls.

The left doll stopped and sneered at him, lifting up the right's hand, fingers still interlocked, and kissed the back. The right doll snickered and Owen blushed.

"Bet this guy would like a show. He's practically drooling."

"Oh, sorry—" Owen began.

"Ugh, why do they let the trolls loose at night?" The left doll rolled his eyes and tugged the other down the street.

Owen's face burned. Wanting nothing more than to be out of sight and back at home, he looked around for a cab. Trolls were monsters that lived under bridges and had a liking for mutton. Trolls couldn't be accountants, couldn't work the number pad of the keyboard with their jagged claws.

Cars passed him by and he headed back to the corner with the subway station. He glanced back over his shoulder now and then. The steps to the station, dingy and wet and reeking of fresh urine, both promised retreat and reminded him that underground was where the trolls hid away from the rest of the world.

He felt guilty for calling in sick the following Monday but he could not bring himself to leave bed except to make his melted sandwich. When he took a bite, the tuna was sour on his tongue.

On his fortieth birthday Owen decided to end his life. His cousins had thrown him a party. He did not recognize most of the faces and the fact that so many strangers wanted to hug him or kiss him or slap his back left him shaking, and too nauseated to do more than pick at his ice cream cake, with its troubling layers of vanilla, *then* chocolate and minty crème, utterly out of proper order.

Owen left their large condo clutching an armful of cards with gift certificates to stores he had never heard of. The moment he'd blown out the garish pink and white wax 4 and 0 candles, Owen knew the future. A life spent alone in his mother's house, a silent phone, a twin bed in which he'd die and not be found for days.

He stopped at the first sewer grate he came to and dropped the cards through the slots into darkness. They made a soft splash into whatever water flowed beneath. The sound, the image, reminded him of stories his mother would tease him with whenever they passed by a sewer. Gigantic albino alligators. She'd also told him that water towers imprisoned immense squid.

He wished one of those alligators—aligrators, he had called them as a child—would burst through a manhole and crunch his old bones. There was never a monster around when you wanted. The thought stayed with him.

He didn't walk back to his apartment. Instead, he wandered until he came upon the old public library he'd visited in grade school. He missed the card catalog. He asked the librarian for help finding monsters. The books she found him reminded Owen of his mother's sofa, with their plastic dust jackets. But they were filled with photos of Frankenstein's Monster or Jack Pierce's other masterpieces. Creatures of greasepaint and celluloid. He needed real fangs.

Working the computer terminal, he found his quarry in 398. Folklore. He pulled out his pocket notebook in which he kept track of his daily, weekly, and monthly expenses, and tore off the first few pages. He wrote down the names and locales of the most promising creatures. Exotic names like *chupacabra* and *jentilak* filled him with excitement. He renewed his membership and checked out a stack of books.

The next day, bleary-eyed from too little sleep after a night of feverish reading, Owen went to work to type out his resignation. He sent it in via email after making the travel arrangements.

=

"Monsters?"

Owen nodded and tapped the book by his plate. "Old stories tell that a hag lives in a cave on the mountain. She has two mouths," he said and clicked his own jaws. "The second is hidden in her hair. She lures lost travelers and devours them."

Saul chuckled. "I would have guessed you were a businessman. Not a Van Helsing."

That distracted Owen for a moment; he would have liked to have been a Cushing Van Helsing more than a Van Sloan Van Helsing but doubted he had either's character.

"So what monsters have you slain?"

"None. I've searched everywhere. England. Scotland and Russia—"

"Where in Russia? I spent six months all over Perm Krai. I camped in the Urals."

Owen had never known anyone who had lived out of a tent for six days let alone months. Such a life, unfettered with a numerical address or zip code, seemed terrifying.

"You're really a professor, right? Studying folklore? I heard this part of Japan has some interesting history."

"I look like a professor?" Owen looked down at himself. His sports coat had seen better days. He imagined tweed patched at the elbows and smiled.

Saul shrugged. He stuffed rice into his mouth. Owen watched his Adam's apple bob with each swallow. Saul had a scrawny neck and several dark hairs peeked out of the collar of his t-shirt. Owen wondered how they would feel. Wiry or soft?

"I taught statistics at Princeton." Owen amazed himself with the lie.

Saul devoured his slices of pickle and Owen offered him the remaining pieces from his own plate. "And you're here because of this—"

"The Yama-uba."

Saul laughed. "I think that's what Japanese kids call grunge chic."

"The stories don't say what she wears." Owen looked at the faded cloth cover of the book.

"So you believe she exists?"

"The law of averages. I've looked for monsters everywhere. One of them has to be real."

Saul reached over the table and took hold of Owen's jacket lapel. He lifted it aide. "Are you packing silver bullets?"

Owen tried to hide his blush with an extra long sip of tea.

"Well, good luck with your hunt." Saul wiped his mouth, then left a rumpled napkin in the center of his plate. "Maybe I'll see you later. If you need an assistant who knows almost nothing about the countryside."

Owen took too long to answer. Saul had left. Owen didn't know how to tell that, just once, he wished to be the one hunted.

=

AT NABEKURA, OWEN avoided the paved road leading up the mountainside. It seemed likely that monsters had an aversion to macadam and steel and glass. He imagined the industrial revolution stranded them like polar bears in the shrinking artic. The Yama-uba might not have fed in decades. She might have withered away to bones frosted with the region's famous white dew.

He flipped through the pages of the library book. They were so brittle with age that corners cracked and fell like eggshell. He didn't seem able to focus on the words. If the Yama-uba proved to be another hoax, he didn't know what he'd do next. He couldn't conceive of a day after. The thought of being alive tomorrow filled him with dread.

He reached into his jacket pocket for a snack and remembered Saul's hand slipping past his lapel. Had that been a flirtation?

Owen clutched the packet of Cool Fran Lemon Biscuit Sticks. He marveled at their sweet smell, sweeter than any lemon ought to be; if he had never come to Japan to die, he would have never discovered so many treats. Though the chocolate he had purchased in Andreapol had been wondrous too. The Brosno dragon never rose from the lake but Owen had enjoyed the mild weather and the Babaevsky bars.

The beech trees on the mountain wore a golden-bronze raiment and whispered in a breeze that grew as the sun lowered to the horizon.

Owen moved higher. He rewarded exertion every so often with another biscuit. They crunched beneath his jaws. *Like tiny bones. I'm a troll snacking on bones*, he thought.

"Most people take the road."

He turned around. A Japanese girl stood in the shade. Long black bangs concealed her eyes. She wore layers and layers of clothing. Owen counted two stringy scarves, an overcoat with pale fur trim, stratum of stockings with holes and socks showing beneath. Her *zori* crushed fallen leaves with their wooden soles.

"Scared you?" She stepped closer. Old-style headphones, the kind sold with old reel-to-reel players, lay atop the scarves around her neck.

"Startled would be more correct."

The girl, who might have been fourteen, fifteen, tapped her chin. "Don't litter."

"I won't." Guilty, he made a show of crumpling the empty package and putting it into his pocket.

"Good. The *kami* wouldn't like it."

"*Kami?*" The word sounded familiar.

She looked up the mountain a moment. "Spirits. If you believe in that sort of thing."

"I'm looking for one of them. The Yama-uba."

She giggled and repeated the name.

Owen's cheeks flushed and he felt foolish, as if he had stopped and asked her for directions.

"Why her?" she asked.

Owen shook his head and started hiking. The girl called out her question again. He answered without turning around. "Most people don't like being mocked."

"You're too late. She's gone."

He stopped and slid back a little. "Gone?" He muttered the word at first. "Gone?" He heard the girl climbing after him.

"Yes."

"As in dead?" He imagined a heap of bones forgotten on the mountainside.

The girl's eyes widened for a moment and she seemed ready to break into another bout of laughter. "No, no, no. She went to the city. Moriokashi. Or maybe Tokyo. It doesn't matter."

"How—"

"You really do want to find her." The idea seemed to perplex her and she stuck the frayed end of one scarf into the corner of her mouth. Her tongue was very pink.

"You're not some director are you? She's not like those *yūrei* in J-horror. I hate those."

"But you've seen her..." Owen didn't know whether he should be thrilled to have finally found a monster to be real or disappointed that he'd arrived too late.

"She raised me. I ran away years ago." The girl pointed up the mountain. "Her cave is not far from here."

"I came all the way from Jersey," Owen said. He felt about to topple, as if his left foot wanted to take another step while the right wanted to turn back.

"Did she eat someone you know?"

"Not quite." Owen took out his notebook. He didn't know whether to cross out the last entry or not.

The girl must have turned on an mp3 player in her pocket because he heard noise coming from her headphones. He didn't care for popular music and couldn't understand why anyone would enjoy something that sounded like eerie whispers and smacking lips. "I could show you the cave. *Her* cave."

He shook his head. What would be the point?

She looked hurt and nibbled more at her scarf. Watching her do so threatened Owen's gag reflex. He imagined the girl living in a hole in the ground, gnawed bones shoved off to the side, kanji scratched on the walls. No wonder she dressed and acted so peculiar. "Why stay? I mean, if she's gone you're free to leave."

"Where would I go? I know the smell of the stone when it rains and the feel of the dirt at my back. When I'm there I can close my eyes and still see everything." Her response sounded petulant. "Every time I step out, there's this tiny voice, echoing my own. It tells me to go back. It's safe and solid, sleeping in the earth. Like my hair and fingers become roots sinking into the ground."

The way she talked about the cave made Owen's chest tighten. "Sometimes being safe is stifling." But after he said it, he remembered that his quest had failed. He'd have to return to America, to Trenton and his mother's house and retreat to his bedroom. He heard himself wheezing, trying to breathe.

He waited for the girl to walk away. But she didn't. They both stood there in awkward silence for a while.

"In all the books I've read about monsters, the authors always mention how man is afraid of the unknown. They even capitalize it. The Unknown. But they're wrong. I'm more afraid of what I expect, what I know I'll be doing tomorrow and the next day." He licked his lips. "And the next. I'd rather have a bit of the Unknown, anything but the Given."

The girl chewed her scarf harder for a moment. "Would you help me carry some things I want from the cave?"

He nodded and moved slowly to follow her.

He stopped when the brush rustled off to his right. A strong breeze? He couldn't be sure. Perhaps a squirrel, if they had them in Japan. He stopped to peer through the beech trees.

The girl called down to him but he remained there. She tramped back down to where he stood. Her music had grown louder.

"Thought I saw a *kami*," he said with a grin.

Her face turned pale like milk. He almost laughed at how scared she looked. The dreary tune quieted for a couple of seconds, as if it had skipped a beat.

When she turned her head to look where he had, Owen took a step behind her. She was no taller than his chest. He couldn't resist teasing her as his mother had done to him. "You're not looking the right way." He brought his hands to her face, covering her eyes, while he smiled. Then he glanced down at the top of her head.

There was no mp3, no radio, making the hungry whispers. In her scalp a pair of leathery lips split and showed teeth sharper, more numerous, than a shark's. Fetid breath blew up and spittle slicked the surrounding hair.

Both Owen and the girl stayed motionless.

Owen felt cold, exposed, as if the temperature had suddenly dropped to freezing. Why couldn't he see his breath? Or hers, rising from between his fingers and rising from her scalp into his eyes. The fear that filled him made all his past anxieties seem like laughter. He could feel the muscles and tendons, nerves and bones within his hands, his entire body, recoiling, seeking to push away from the girl, this thing's body. But his hands refused to move.

He bit back the scream. Thoughts of dying sweated out of his every pore.

He clamped his hands tighter around her head. She said something in Japanese but his palm muffled her lower mouth. Then he twisted, hard, to the right. The snap sounded like stepping on a branch. The Yama-uba went limp against him. A soft sigh escaped her lips.

Owen let her fall to the ground. His hands trembled. He hugged them in his armpits. His teeth chattered.

The exposed skin of the Yama-uba's hands and neck grew loose, like dripping wax, then congealed in wrinkled folds. The nails long and yellowed and split. But her face, from smooth brow to rounded cheek and slight chin, her face remained a young girl's.

In movies, the monsters always looked different when they died, even poor Lawrence Talbot. He turned away from the body. He could not stand the sight of her face, serene despite the open stare.

He stumbled down the mountainside. Sometimes he fell and slid, ripping and staining his clothes. He almost collapsed when he saw the dark ribbon of the roadway. He sat down by the side of the road and put his head between his knees.

He wasn't sure how much time had passed when someone tapped him on the shoulder. He hesitated to look up, knowing, somehow, that he would see the Yama-uba's youthful face. But the thick mustached man who stood over him and spoke a rush of German looked concerned. Owen offered a weak smile that satisfied whatever Samaritan instinct the tourist possessed.

Owen stood up. When he brushed himself off, he felt the slight bulge of his notebook in a pocket. He slipped it out and turned to the final entry. He became annoyed when he thought he'd lost his pen, and then saw it by his feet. A sense of accomplishment filled him as he crossed out *Yama-uba*. No monsters after Y.

Then a cold draft of air brought a thought. Yeti. For a moment, Owen envisioned himself covered in thick furs and climbing snow-covered cliffs. A handsome Sherpa showed him tracks before suggesting they rest for the night. Sharing a tent, of course, to keep warm.

Sharing a tent with someone like Saul.

He almost wrote it down. Instead he scribbled in the word *Troll*, then crossed it out with a grin and headed back to town. He left the notebook behind.

AUTHOR'S NOTE

So the last story. The last Author Note. A great many of my fears are part of the fabric of "A Troll on a Mountain with a Girl." The earlier drafts were darker but as the misery poured out of me onto the page, I realized I needed more than a different ending. I needed a different story. And so Saul (a name my mother wanted for me) was given one.

Maybe one day I will allow myself the same luxury.

Stories demand that characters make wrong decisions. If they never stray from the path, never enter those dark woods, then the plot languishes. Lately, I've become aware that I make bad decisions in perverse anticipation of telling friends the mishaps I imagine will follow afterwards. I suppose this is a bit of meta-masochism for a writer, to be so willing to step into the role of character despite knowing what harm might come.

Years ago, while working on my first serious attempt to write a novel, a low fantasy, I devised this creed by which the protagonist segregated society. What would you want to know about a stranger? His secret? His story? Or his weakness? He was a thorn, a spy, and only cared for secrets. If a person answered weakness he thought them an oaf, story he considered them a fool. I then realized that, by my character's standards, I was an immense one.

But now I see the question is flawed. Characters need their secrets and weaknesses. I've become the romantic and see the merit of all three.

Now, do you know my secret? My weakness?

Let me tell you a story...

ACKNOWLEDGEMENTS

THANKS TO THE kind editors that believed these stories belonged on the page: Ellen Datlow, Ken Furtado, Greg Herren, Richard Labonté, Ekaterina Sedia, Cecilia Tan, Paul Tremblay, Sean Wallace, and Terri Windling.

I may owe a debt to sanofi-aventis for Ambien. I can't recall.

Further thanks to devoted and generous friends who had the patience to read word after word, from madcap scribble to last moment revision: Chris Barzak, Holly Black, Rick Bowes, Robert Levy, Kelly Link, Livia Llewellyn, Will Ludwigsen, Aimee Payne, Sherwood Smith, Wayne Wilkening and the indispensable Ann Zeddies. Your persistence allowed me to realize what I sought within the stories themselves.

I definitely owe a debt to Daulton, who reminded me that a nap, no matter the time of day, does wonders.

Additional thanks to Toby Johnson and Matthew Bright, who suffered through the production of this book.

The greatest debt is owed to my parents—I envy their skill at telling me I love you in so many ways.

ABOUT THE AUTHOR

Steve Berman happens to have many crowded shelves of books and odd toys and plush creatures. He's been a finalist for the Andre Norton, Lambda Literary, and the Gaylactic Spectrum Awards. He worries if he could find shelf space for any of these, if he ever won.

One of his favorite sounds is a cat's purr.